"I'm going to the Emporium. You have the number. If there's trouble, call. I can be back in five minutes," Stevie said firmly.

"I'm already in trouble," Hal growled under his breath.

She got no farther than the hall before she felt his hand on her arm, propelling her into the office. "You're not going anywhere; you're staying here with me, until we work this out," Hal informed her with a dangerous glint in his eyes, pressing her back against the wall, pushing her pulse into overdrive. "I'll fight with you if you want to fight. I'll make love with you if you want to make love. But I'm through letting you pretend I'm not here. So what's it going to be, Stevie Lee?" he demanded. "Loving or fighting?"

The sultry roughness of his voice left no doubt about which answer he preferred and left her scrambling for a shred of composure. One more kiss and she'd never survive with her heart intact.

"Fighting," she whispered, looking at the floor, the desk, anywhere but into those truth-seeking indigo eyes.

"Wrong answer, sweetheart, but I'll give you another shot." In one smooth move he pulled her hat off her head, letting it fall to the floor, and ran his fingers through her hair.

"Hal—" The warmth of his touch raced across her skin, and his gentleness melted another layer of her protective ice. As she lifted her eyes to his, he caught a fleeting moment of desire she hadn't been able to hide.

"Stevie, I don't know why you're running so fast and hard . . . but you'll never run fast enough or hard enough to get away from me. . . ."

WHAT ARE *LOVESWEPT* ROMANCES?

They are stories of true romance and touching emotion. We believe those two very important ingredients are constants in our highly sensual and very believable stories in the *LOVESWEPT* line. Our goal is to give you, the reader, stories of consistently high quality that may sometimes make you laugh, sometimes make you cry, but are always fresh and creative and contain many delightful surprises within their pages.

Most romance fans read an enormous number of books. Those they truly love, they keep. Others may be traded with friends and soon forgotten. We hope that each *LOVESWEPT* romance will be a treasure—a "keeper." We will always try to publish

LOVE STORIES YOU'LL NEVER FORGET
BY AUTHORS YOU'LL ALWAYS REMEMBER

The Editors

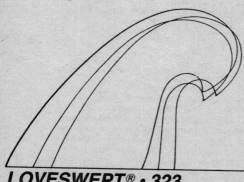

LOVESWEPT® • 323

Glenna McReynolds
Stevie Lee

 BANTAM BOOKS
TORONTO • NEW YORK • LONDON • SYDNEY • AUCKLAND

To Mary and Wayne with love.
Thanks for sharing your little piece
of paradise.

STEVIE LEE

A Bantam Book / April 1989

*If you would be interested in receiving protective vinyl
covers for your Loveswept books, please write to this address
for information:*

Loveswept
Bantam Books
P.O. Box 985
Hicksville, NY 11802

ISBN 0-553-21974-X

Published simultaneously in the United States and Canada

PRINTED IN THE UNITED STATES OF AMERICA

O   0 9 8 7 6 5 4 3 2 1

One

Halsey Morgan was alive—bad news sure traveled fast.

Stevie Lee Brown held the telephone receiver at arm's length and gave it a long, hard look, barely fighting the temptation to rip the darn thing off the wall. Ten lousy calls in the last four hours had all reported the same lousy news—Halsey Morgan was alive. From the Grand Lake postmaster to the station attendant at the Gas 'Em Up, everybody wanted to extend their sympathies.

"Halsey Morgan," she muttered, finally hanging up the phone in disgust. With the unconscious ease of habit, she slumped against the beer cooler and absently wiped her hands on the bar towel wrapped around her waist. Dampness stained the front of her worn jeans. Loose strands of honey-brown hair clung to her cheeks and trailed down the front of her red shirt, adding to her mussed and tired appearance.

Sure as the sun rising in the morning, she was

doomed to spend the rest of her days in this backwater wilderness tucked up against the Rocky Mountains. The Trail's End Bar actually would be the end of her trail. The same old faces, the same old gossip year after year, she thought, and all thanks to a miraculously resurrected Halsey Morgan. Obviously the rumors about his death in the South Pacific had been just that—rumors. If half of the rest of what she'd heard about his exploits was true, he should have been dead a long time ago. But he wasn't, and now her plans were ruined.

"Hey! Stevie! What's a guy gotta do to get a drink around here?" A booming male voice carried the question into the semidarkened hall.

A weary sigh escaped her lips. Too tired to kick the man out, she crossed her arms and leaned harder into the beer cooler to wait him out. How she'd ever allowed Kong Kingman to overdrink was beyond her. Sure, she'd had a lot on her mind, but only a fool would let the behemoth of Grand County get snockered in her bar, and the one thing Stevie prided herself on was being nobody's fool.

"Hey! I know you're back there!" Kong hollered again. Of course she was there, she thought irritably, tucking her hands further under her arms. She was always back there, cleaning up, serving up, and dishing out.

Damn that Halsey Morgan anyway.

Halsey had gotten himself another bargain, that was for certain. Why he didn't invest in a real car instead of always picking up somebody else's lemon was beyond him; or rather, it was beyond his financial situation. Everything was beyond his financial situation. Delilah had sucked him dry.

He dropped the last of his groceries into the bed of the pickup truck and wrestled a tarp over them to keep out the high country blizzard. Heavy gusts of wind whipped his hair and chilled his face. His half-frozen fingers struggled with a length of climbing rope.

It was springtime in the Rockies, when Mother Nature let loose with her whole bag of tricks from blizzards to thunderstorms, rolling them all up into one and throwing them across the night sky. Bolts of lightning danced behind the low-hanging clouds. Thunder rumbled across the Kawuneeche Valley and echoed off the Never Summer Range. The beauty and power of the display got his blood going; Mom Nature was good at that. She'd stolen his heart at a very young age, and she'd never let go.

He slip-knotted the rope, then jumped in the cab and slammed the door a couple of times until it caught. Each attempt deposited a fresh layer of snow on the seat, and tightened his mouth another degree toward grim. He didn't need this kind of trouble, not after what he'd been through. People had been looking at him funny all day, setting his nerves on edge. Halsey wasn't a common name, but the wide-eyed, slack-jawed response of the Grand Lake postmaster had made him wonder if it was stranger than he thought. He hoped not. He needed to figure out a way to make a living in this town, which meant getting a job—which wasn't likely if everyone he ran into looked at him funny.

With equal amounts of cussing and praying, he turned the key and waited through the truck's prerequisite coughing and hacking. When the engine finally caught, a flicker of a smile crossed his mouth. "Just get me home." He gave the dash a solid pat.

Home. The word had a foreign sound in his mind. He'd spent too many years in faraway places, he thought as he wiggled and shook the gearshift into first—and too many months stuck on that island where even the greatest boat builder in the world couldn't have put back together what the South Pacific had taken apart.

Hal didn't know what the rest of the world had called the maelstrom of wind and water that had swallowed his sailboat and spat it out on a strange and desolate shore, but he called the storm 'Delilah,' the lady who had laid him low. If a cruising yachtsman hadn't spotted the wreckage, he'd still be rotting away under the coconut palms, living on sushi, and trying to rig together everything that could float. The episode had put a slight crimp in his adventuresome spirit and a major fracture in his bankroll. He told himself he was damn lucky to be back in the good old U.S. of A., told himself he was glad to be home—but he wished like hell he still had *Freedom* under his feet with the wind in her sails.

Instead what he had under his feet was a worn-out clutch and a gas pedal that went through the floorboard. He'd never seen the likes of it. A rainstorm in Utah had soaked him to the knees, and now his legs were encased in a thin layer of icy cotton.

Yessiree, he thought with a wry grin, *darn glad to be back in the good old U.S. of A.* Maybe he should have a drink to celebrate his return before heading back to the cabin.

As if seconding his thoughts, the engine groaned and choked. Hal slammed down on the clutch and gave the truck more gas. The damn thing loved gas. Hal doubted if they'd missed a station between the West Coast and the Continental Divide. The engine warmed up in spits and jerks, and then, out of the blue, it died. Not a hesitant death, not in the least. Nope. Hal had enough experience to know when an engine left for the great beyond, and his just had.

Wonderful. He slumped over the steering wheel, muttering every dockside obscenity he knew. The list took a couple of minutes to complete and did little to ease his anger. Now, besides needing a drink, he needed a ride home.

Fat chance, he thought. The grocery clerk had locked the door behind him and was probably long gone. He glanced out the windows for another sign of life in the deserted mountain town and found only one.

TRAIL'S END . . . TRAIL'S END, a flash of blue neon glowed at the end of the block, backlighting the flurries of wind-driven snow. He sighed. This wasn't at all how he'd imagined his end of the trail. An ice crevasse on Mount Everest maybe, or getting "Maytagged" in a stretch of white water, but not freezing to death in the middle of Grand Lake, Colorado.

A wry smile curved a corner of his mouth again and stuck. *Trail's End.* If he wasn't so tired and hungry, the situation would be funny. But there wasn't anything funny about freezing to death, so he hauled himself out of the cab and began the cold walk to the Trail's End Bar.

•　•　•

"He looks a little rough around the edges, Stevie. I wouldn't want to tangle with him."

Stevie heard her older sister's summation of Halsey Morgan through the buzz and crackle of the phone line and let out another heavy sigh before answering. "I don't plan on tangling with him, Nola. If he's got the money to get his property out of hock, fine. If not, I'll pay the taxes on it again this year and it will be mine. All legal. All tidy." *All shot to hell in a hand basket*, she added silently, doubting if Mr. Morgan had any intention of losing his cabin and acreage to back taxes. What a sweet deal it had been.

"Well, he didn't look as though he had much money." Nola's voice lifted hopefully.

"His kind never do." But his kind managed to wander the world freely, which was more than Stevie could manage. No one could tell her he didn't have something stashed away.

"Dried beans, generic coffee, a loaf of bread, a dozen eggs, ten pounds of potatoes, peanut butter, no jelly . . ."

Stretching the phone cord behind her, Stevie walked over to the window and pressed her nose against the glass. "Nola?" she asked, interrupting the rundown of Morgan's grocery list. "Why are you telling me this?" A snowplow turned onto the main street and lowered its blade. Great, she thought, she shouldn't have too much trouble getting home. Her Mustang had chains, but she wasn't up to putting them on tonight.

"And three of those little boxes of macaroni and cheese," Nola added, finishing the list. "Isn't it obvious? The man is broke. Your position is secure."

That was a pretty big leap of logic, even for

Nola, Stevie thought as she walked back to the beer cooler and rested against the door. The phone line hummed and buzzed through the silence in typical backwoods style, even though the call originated less than two blocks away.

"Okay," her sister finally conceded. "I'm sorry, honey. We all know how much you were counting on . . . well, on Halsey Morgan being dead or something."

Unvarnished with particulars, the truth sounded awful, and Stevie felt an immediate pang of guilt. That it was her first pang all day only increased her unease. Ridiculous, she chided herself, trying to brush the emotion aside. Most people wouldn't last a week doing the things Halsey Morgan did year in and year out, but then Halsey Morgan wasn't most people.

From the Himalayas to the Amazon Basin, he'd blazed a trail of danger and adventure. When he had first disappeared in the South Pacific, some folks had believed he'd be found, hale and hearty, soaking up French Polynesian sunshine on one of the outer islands. They had discounted his disappearance as a mere breakdown in communications. "Halsey Morgan," they said, "followed his own star." Skeptics, like Stevie, usually added, "—right off the edge of the earth."

When a piece of his boat had washed up on Pukapuka, or Bora Bora, or wherever, the skeptics had congratulated Stevie on her foresight in attempting to buy up his tax-delinquent property. But foresight was hardly the word Stevie would have used. Desperation had been her motivation, one last desperate chance to get out of debt, and out of town. This backwater wilderness had held her captive for a lifetime, which was long enough in her book.

"Hey! Stevie! We need another beer here!" Kong bellowed.

We? Stevie glanced over her shoulder. The last time she'd checked, Kong had been alone. From the hallway she caught a glimpse of another man's back. Maybe if she ignored him, he'd go away. She'd planned on kicking Kong out as soon as she hung up. Staying open for two late-night loners was a waste of electricity—and she already had two pink slips from the power company. One more and she'd be pouring beer in the dark.

"I better get going, Nola. Kong's shouting down the rafters."

"Well, you just tell him to hold his horses. That boy probably has enough beer stored up in that gut of his to float a battleship."

"Yeah, and most of it's mine." Stevie opened the beer refrigerator with her free hand. She wanted to finish up and go home. She mentally tallied up the stock. A case of Bud, half a case of Molson's, a couple of Hussong's . . .

"Are you coming to Sunday supper?" Nola asked.

"Stevie Lee!" Kong bellowed.

Stevie quietly sighed. "Not this Sunday, Nola, and you won't be there either. It's Memorial Day, remember? There'll be tons of people in town buying groceries and booze. Be sure to remind Mom."

"Oh, gosh! I forgot. Oh, honey, I've got to go. I need to double my order. Bye." The phone clicked in her ear.

Yep, a real helluva night, Stevie thought, giving the receiver a wry look. Then she hung up and walked back to the storeroom. With luck, both of her customers would be gone by the time she refilled the cooler.

Hal watched the hairy giant of a man ease himself off the bar stool, squeeze himself behind the bar, and lumber into the dark hallway. Hopefully he'd come back with the unknown Stevie in tow. And hopefully the bartender would give him a ride home. One look at the big guy weaving on his bar stool had convinced Hal not to approach him for the needed favor—that and the suspicion that the wreck parked out front belonged to him. The car had seen its share of the bottoms of ditches.

On the other hand, the Mustang out front was a dream on wheels. Even half-frozen, he'd taken a moment to run his hand over the cherry-red paint job with white flames scorching the sides and the word "Dynamite" swirled across the back panel. She was somebody's baby all right. With a little luck, she'd also be his ride home.

Hal stepped closer to the stone fireplace to warm his backside and looked around the Trail's End. Small and shabby, it reminded him of a hundred others he'd seen all over the world, a locals' bar. A dart board hung next to the fireplace, but only someone standing behind the bar could have gotten enough distance on a dart to hit it. Sure enough, he thought as his gaze roamed the shelves of liquor on the far wall and found the darts in a box between the bottles. The board was there for the bartenders, not the customers. It was strange but not surprising, considering the lack of business. Maybe if they fixed the place up, they'd do better. In return for a ride, he'd offer his handyman services for a day.

A thudding sound drew his attention to the dark hallway. He listened for a second and, when no other noise was forthcoming, went back to looking around. He could fix the broken table stashed in the corner, the busted shelf behind the bar, the ripped vinyl on the booths flanking both sides of the front door.

The sound of glass breaking snapped his head back toward the hall. Curiosity almost propelled him forward, but the fire was warm, and once again no other sound followed the second. He brushed off the crash by deciding the unknown Stevie had stupidly entrusted the big drunk with something breakable. He returned his attention to the bar. Maybe he'd offer to clean the smoke and soot off the fireplace. Then again, he thought, his cabin was only five miles out of town, a distance which shouldn't demand too many hours of repayment.

A muffled sound came next, hitting a wrong chord in his mind, and Hal moved forward a couple of steps. Then a woman screamed.

Two

Stevie strangled out her next cry. Two hundred and thirty pounds of amorous ape pressed her backward over the desk, sending papers and ledgers flying in all directions.

"Come on, Stevie"—his breath was enough to make her faint— "lay those lips on me, honey."

"Ah . . . ah," she couldn't breathe. Her right hand slapped the desk behind her in a frantic search for something to hit him with. The adding machine fell under her grasp. *Not the adding machine, Stevie!* She kept searching, and gasping.

"Sweet, sweet, Stevie Lee," he crooned, his hand groping up her leg.

That did it. She went back for the piece of office equipment, wrapping her fingers around the side and swinging it up in a desperate arc. But before she could connect it with his head, he released her. Stevie slid to the floor with a thump. Kong was less than a second behind her.

Pulse racing, lungs burning, she stared at the

mountain of man sprawled on the floor in front of her. What in the world had gotten into him? And what in the world had happened to him? she wondered. Had he had a heart attack? A stroke? Passed out?

"Are you okay?"

Stevie's head jerked up at the sound of a rough, masculine voice—and her heart stopped for an eternally long instant. Never, ever, not even in her wildest dreams had she seen anyone like the man towering over her.

Standing in the rubble strewn across the floor, he blocked the light with his broad shoulders and powerfully built body, an ancient warrior come to life. Shaggy, golden hair swept away from his shadowed face like a lion's mane, layering over the quilted fabric of a white parka. One of his hands was still clenched into a fist, the imprint of which she was sure she'd find on Kong's jaw.

Speechlessly, Stevie followed the dark line of his T-shirt down to a bright silver buckle and a pair of ragged jeans hanging low on his hips. A thigh-length tear in the denim revealed thickly corded muscles beneath the dark, bare skin of his left leg. Melting ice dampened the lower half of his pants and pooled around his scuffed, heavy boots.

"Are you okay?" he repeated, hunkering down on one knee and filling her world with the barest of smiles and strangely compelling dark blue eyes.

Okay? she wondered, her own eyes widening in disbelief; she couldn't even breathe. *Halsey Morgan was alive.* The mountains outside were beautiful and strong, and this man had the same natural beauty—clean and pure, and as wild as the places he'd seen, as untamed as the mountains he'd climbed. Pale lines, no doubt caused by days of squinting into the sun over an endless sea, feathered the corners of his eyes. The broad, masculine features of his face were burnt brown by the same tropical sun, a rich dark color shining with vitality.

". . . and I thought you were dead," she whispered, unable to take her eyes off him.

"Yeah, well, a lot of people probably wrote me off. It's not the first time." His easy grin broadened into a dazzling smile. The heat of it warmed the faraway depths of his eyes, and melted Stevie's socks.

Whoa . . . The thought slipped through the back alleys of her mind, catching at her heart and slowing her pulse to a long cadence. His was a midnight smile, the kind you wanted to find on the pillow next to yours when the world was dark and quiet. The kind you wanted to feel against your throat while he whispered something, anything, against your skin.

Hal read the emotions as they crossed her face, and what they told him triggered every sensual avenue in his body. There were a lot of things he wasn't ready to face yet: Freeway traffic, junk food, and anything resembling a shopping mall. But in the space of a breath, he realized how ready he was for a woman, this woman.

Silky waves of hair tumbled over her shoulders, half in and half out of the braid hanging to her waist. The honey-brown ribbon draped across her full breasts and bisected the word "Dynamite" embroidered on the clingy, red cotton of her shirt. Silently he agreed. She was pure dynamite.

She'd spoken as if she knew him, but one look at her face—creamy skin blushed by the sun, a full wide mouth, and clear gray eyes shadowed by nothing more than her thick, dark lashes—and he knew he never would have forgotten her. All those hours on the beach, dreaming of the pleasure of a woman in his arms, were coming back to him with an intensity he was finding hard to resist.

Stevie felt the slow, heated track of his gaze lingering on her breasts. She felt his eyes on her like a touch as they drifted to her face, and she knew the time had long since passed when she should have gotten a grip, any kind of a grip on herself. But it was too late.

Gently, he reached out and cupped her chin in his palm. The warmth of his hand, the brush of his thumb below her mouth, caused her lips to part and her heart to stop.

The slight gesture was all the encouragement he needed. He leaned forward, pulling her closer, the golden length of his hair slipping over his shoulder and melding with hers. For a moment, his lips grazed her cheek, warming her skin; then his mouth claimed hers, lightly, sweetly.

Her soft intake of breath told him of her surprise, and her hesitation—and the even softer feel of her mouth told him of her willingness. Hal knew what he was doing was wrong, but it didn't stop him from running his hand along the curve of her jaw, tunneling his fingers through the silkiness of her hair, and losing himself in the tender delight of her kiss.

From the outside in, all of Stevie's awareness pooled into the lazy, sensual track of his mouth over hers, leaving no place for her shock to take hold. She raised her hand to his shoulder, meaning to push him away. But the moment she touched him, his tongue slid into her mouth. A hundred emotions instantly collided in her chest and fragmented into a thousand demanding desires. They made her curl her fingers around the downy material of his parka. They forced her mouth open and beckoned to long-forgotten sensations.

Hal felt the emotions coursing through her body, and he wanted nothing more, and nothing less, then to lower her to the floor and ease his months of loneliness away, to rediscover the special joy of a woman, to discover the mysteries of this special woman. But however compliant she seemed in his arms, he knew he'd taken advantage of her in a weak moment and that all too soon, she'd realize it. To save himself from certain condemnation—and maybe a slap in the face, or worse—he slowly pulled himself from her.

When he lifted his head, his eyes were dark, his face flushed beneath his tan. "Sorry about that," he said softly, not sounding the least bit repentant.

Stevie had no such apology to offer. Halsey Morgan was definitely, incredibly alive. Her lips tingled with the knowledge. His body, so hard beneath her hands, so close to hers, tempted her to pull him back down for another kiss.

Get that grip, Stevie, or you're going to make a fool out of yourself. The voice of reason stayed her hand in the nick of time.

"I need a drink." She choked the words out around the huge lump of embarrassment forming in her throat. What was going on in this town tonight? she wondered. Had the storm unleashed everybody's primal urges? First Kong, then Halsey Morgan. She hadn't seen this much action since . . . since she didn't know when. Her knees trembled as she struggled to her feet. Nobody hit on

Stevie Lee Brown; that was rule number one—and it had just been busted up and tossed around like so much confetti. "I really need a drink," she repeated more forcefully.

"Sounds good." He smiled and rose with her, helping her with a hand around her arm. "What about him?" He nodded at the sprawling giant.

Stevie followed his gesture, took one look, and said, "I think he's had enough." Then she stepped over the size-fourteen logging boots and made a beeline for the bar.

Hal's grin broadened from ear to ear as he followed her through the narrow hall. The lady had remarkable recuperative powers. She also had a remarkable body. Somehow, he'd forgotten how a pair of stone-washed jeans looked on a pair of long legs belonging to someone of the feminine gender. This lady had just reminded him in no uncertain terms—they looked great. His appreciative gaze told him the term "Dynamite" had more to do with the way she put one foot in front of the other than with anything under the hood of the Mustang. And her kiss? Well, her kiss defied any comparison on either side of any ocean. His grin broadened. The end of the trail had never looked, or felt, so good.

How did she get into these messes? Stevie wondered, holding her head with one hand and groping in the well for the whiskey bottle with the other. Finding it, she poured herself a healthy shot and finished it in one long swallow. Her nose wrinkled as she set the glass back on the bar. She preferred gin, but gin made her crazy. Years ago she'd figured out it must be all those juniper berries used to flavor the gin. Once, in a fancy restaurant down in Denver, she'd seen a high-priced item on the menu that was made with juniper berries. She'd steered clear of it too.

But she'd done a darn poor job of steering clear of Halsey Morgan. She heard him come up behind her, and a jolt of panic stopped her heart cold. For an everlasting moment, she held her breath, her hand tightening on the shot glass. On a night as crazy as this one had been, anything that happened once could easily happen twice.

His heavy boots creaked across the old wooden floor step by step but thankfully kept going to the other side of the bar. Best place for him, she thought with relief, following him out of the corner of her eye, not at all sure what to do about him. Stevie Lee Brown wasn't used to being rescued, and she sure wasn't used to being kissed, by anyone, not in a long time—and never the way he'd kissed her.

Barely refortified by the whiskey, she waited for him to sit down. "What's your pleasure?" she asked, straining to keep her voice steady.

The immediate quirk of his mouth gave the familiar request an entirely new meaning, and much to her dismay, she felt an equally immediate reaction—the faint heat of a blush stealing over her cheeks.

She wanted to run and hide from the teasing glint in his eyes, from her own emotional confusion. Instead she reached way down deep inside herself for the strength to hold his gaze. He'd already breached far, far too many of her invisible barriers, and the few she had left were dangerously close to buckling under. Had she really allowed him to kiss her? To touch his mouth to hers? To hold her?

"Wh-what would you like to drink?" she stam-

mered into the silence, needing desperately to take
some kind of control.

He was still smiling, and Stevie wished he'd
stop. Then maybe she could get her brain back in
working order.

"Whatever you're having is fine," he replied, easing down on a bar stool.

His acquiescence, however slight, gave her confidence a boost. "Not quite. The man who punched
out Kong Kingman deserves better than well liquor. How about a shot of Chivas?" she asked,
but inside she wondered if his voice had always
been so gravelly, or if the tropical sun had burned
the softness out of it the same way it had burned
the color out of his hair. The comparatively bright
light in the bar showed a darker color under the
white-blond, a sable-brown to match his eyebrows
and the hair feathering over his ears.

When he said "Fine," she picked the bottle off
the shelf.

"Kong Kingman?"

She poured his drink and hesitated, smoothing
a swath of dishevelled hair behind her ear. "Jerry,
actually," she explained. Then she threw caution
to the wind and poured herself another shot—of
the good stuff this time. "But he fancies himself a
big ape, and no one's ever disagreed. Least of all
me, especially tonight. Thanks . . . I owe you." The
admission came hard and caused her heart to
sink a little lower in her chest.

A quick smile tugged at Hal's mouth; the pretty
lady with the deadly curves had given him the
perfect opening. "How about a ride home then?
My truck conked out in the middle of Main Street.
I don't live too far out of town, only about five—"

"County Road Four," she interrupted. At his

nmediate look of confusion, she plowed ahead,
eciding that her best defense in this situation
vas to lay her cards on the table—one at a time,
f course. "We're neighbors. Won't be out of my
vay at all. But even if it was, I'd give you a ride
ome. You saved my—me a pile of trouble. Stevie
ee Brown." She lifted her shot glass in salute.

"Halsey Morgan," he replied, his mouth curving
1to another one of those wonderfully alarming,
1idnight smiles.

"Salud." Stevie quickly dowsed the flutter of her
ulse with a shot of premium Scotch. False cour-
ge, they called it, but Stevie wasn't in any posi-
.on to quibble.

Hal followed suit, wincing as the liquor burned
path down his throat. Months of coconut milk
nd rainwater had hardened him in some ways,
ut obviously softened him in others.

"I don't remember having a neighbor," he said
vhen he found his voice again.

"You didn't the last time you were here. Your
roperty borders my dad's ranch." Her voice didn't
ound the least bit strained by the straight shot
f alcohol. It flowed melodically, her western drawl
·ngthening all of her vowels and slurring the
.arder edges off of her consonants. Hal liked the
ound. "He built the cabin for me two years ago.
m at the top of the meadow, just above your
lace." She paused, taking a deep breath and slant-
1g a wary look up at him from under her lashes.
['ve been—uh—I've been . . . do you want a beer
) chase that with?" she asked in a rush.

"Please." He nodded, wondering what in the
vorld she'd been doing, and why, if it was so
.erve-wracking, she wanted to tell him. She
·eached behind her and scooped a beer mug off

the shelf. For a second he thought she wasn't going to get a grip on it, but she did without even a second glance.

"Light or dark?"

"Dark." Like the lashes shadowing your soft gray eyes, he thought, then instantly wondered where the fanciful thought had come from. Shifting uneasily on the stool, he attempted to steer his mind in another direction. "Have you had a lot of trouble around here with guys like Kong?"

"Only once," she replied, seemingly absorbed in filling the stein. With a practiced move, she floated a cocktail napkin precisely in front of him and landed the beer without spilling a drop.

Despite the slender curves, the long tumble of gold-streaked hair, and the intense memory of the softness of her kiss, Hal believed her. When she spoke, the firm set of her mouth had no-nonsense stamped all over it. He wished he could say the same for his imagination. It was going hog-wild behind the calm exterior of his face, fantasizing about her breasts and legs, and her hair spread out and falling through his fingers.

Say something, Hal, he told himself. *Say something before you do something stupid—like lean over and kiss her again, and this time get yourself coldcocked by a Chivas bottle.*

"So we're neighbors, but we've never met." The slight lift in his voice turned the statement into a question.

"I know you by reputation and exploits, but no, we've never met."

Hal knew there were a few women here and there around the world who latched onto mountain climbers and river runners, looking for vicarious and not so vicarious thrills, but this lady didn't seem the type—which left him still mildly confused.

"And yet you were worried when you thought I was dead?" he asked, lifting the stein to his mouth.

Guileless gray eyes met his squarely, and her sweet, no-nonsense mouth delivered a shocking blow. "Hoping is more like it."

Hal choked on his beer. It sputtered out of his mouth, ran down his chin, and soaked the last dry spot on his body—the front of his shirt.

"Sorry about that." Stevie handed him a bar towel and gave herself a mental kick. Sure, she wanted to be the one to tell him, but even on her worst days she usually showed more tact.

What in the hell had he gotten himself into? Hal wondered, mopping away and feeling like a fool. He'd only been in town one day and already he'd been looked at strangely, lost his only transportation, ended up in a bar fight, and gotten turned on by a woman who wished he was dead. Civilization certainly had taken a turn for the worse since he'd left.

He wiped up the beer pooling in the creases of his jeans, and felt a cold trickle run down his thigh through the ripped cloth. Dammit, he thought, he was half-frozen already. Maybe it was time to call in his debts. Big John still owed him a few plane tickets for the endorsement Hal had given his ski area. He'd ask for one to the other side of the earth. Maybe things would look better down under, where Chauncey Keats would be good for a month of room and board in the outback, considering that Hal had damn near died testing his newfangled tent in Alaska. He'd learned one thing from that venture—never trust an alpine tent built by someone who lived in a desert.

"It's nothing personal." Her soft reassurance broke into his thoughts.

"Nothing personal?" He jerked his head up, his voice rising to an incredulous pitch. "A woman I don't even know wants me dead, and it's nothing personal?"

"I didn't *want* you dead. Lost worked out just as well."

He was lost all right. "What in the hell did I ever do to you?" he asked, dumbfounded.

"Nothing, but lost . . . or dead . . . you're worth about seventy grand to me. On the hoof you're worthless."

Hal slumped back on his bar stool. Worthless? Well that was a fine how-do-you-do from a woman he'd saved from the clutches of a big hairy ape. "You beat all, lady. You really beat all."

"You asked." She shrugged and set another beer in front of him, but Hal wasn't at all sure he wanted it. "Go ahead. It's safe. I wouldn't do you or anybody else in for money. Not even seventy thousand dollars."

Seventy thousand dollars? The thought wrinkled his brow. How could he possibly be worth that kind of money to anyone—dead or alive? Hell, he'd probably have to pay somebody to take that damn truck off his hands, and the only other thing he owned in the whole wide world was . . .

"My cabin," he muttered, narrowing his eyes and pinning her with an accusing glare. "You're after my cabin."

"Not only after it, but almost got it. You haven't paid your taxes in two years." There, she'd done her good deed for the night. It felt awful.

"Taxes?" He looked at her as if she were crazy. "Sorry to disappoint you, lady, but I haven't had any income in two years. Maybe longer. Besides, what do my taxes have to do with you?"

It was Stevie's turn to choke. "Not income taxes. Property taxes." Good Lord, she thought, where had this guy been all his life? Dumb question. All she had to do was pick up any outdoor magazine from the last ten years, and she'd be able to pinpoint his whereabouts at any given time. Unfortunately the only picture she'd seen of him hadn't shown her anything of the man. Typical mountaineering gear included dark glasses, heavy coats, snug hat, and the inevitable ice-encrusted face. Nothing had prepared her for the Nordic god gracing her bar stool.

"Property taxes," he repeated slowly, and she could almost see the lightbulb turn on over his head. "Damn. And you bought them."

"It was all legal, cut-and-dried business. Anybody could have paid them." She shrugged again, her slender shoulders lifting and falling with nonchalance.

The gesture was the final blow to his ego. His last piece of solid financial ground was dust in the wind, and a woman who by all rights should be gazing at him with stars in her eyes was cool as a cucumber.

Hal started thinking fast, a trait he'd relied on more than once when his back was against the wall, or when his life was on the line. This was a definite back-against-the-wall situation, which required only two main ingredients for a foolproof plan—a debt he could call in, and a debtor who had something he wanted. By her own admission, she owed him—and he could think of a hundred things she had that he wanted, but he'd start with a job. From what he'd seen of the town, she was his best bet, and he'd certainly succeeded taking longer shots.

"You know, I almost broke my hand decking that jerk."

Stevie's warning instincts lit up like a dance hall on Saturday night. She didn't know where he was coming from, but she knew the conversation had just taken a sharp turn for the worse. Eyeing him warily, she said, "Thanks again."

"Could have gotten real ugly, real fast, if I hadn't shown up." He tossed the remark off as if it were barely worth mentioning.

"I doubt it," she said. "He's big, but he's dumb. I was just getting ready to hit him myself." It was true, but she doubted if it would have done her much good. She watched him drain his glass.

Hal grinned and almost missed the bar when he lowered his glass. The lady had more *cojones* than most of his past climbing partners. But she was wrong, and it was his duty to tell her.

"Not the way I see it. In this case, I think brawn had it all over brains. Beshides, what do you need my seventy thousand dollars for? You've already got your little piece of paradise." His arm swung out to encompass the whole bar, and his body came darn close to following. Only his well-honed sense of balance kept him on the stool. He'd had something else to say; he was sure of it, but it momentarily had slipped his mind.

Stevie hadn't missed a single slip. He'd made three: Two motor, one verbal. A slow, easy smile lifted a corner of her mouth. She'd seen it happen before—people coming up from sea level getting drunk on half their normal intake of alcohol in the rarified altitude of the Rockies. Halsey Morgan had definitely come up from sea level—and he was definitely going down fast. Nola had been wrong; her little sister Stevie was going to handle this guy just fine . . . *as long as he didn't kiss her.*

Stevie unconsciously dismissed the wayward thought with a flick of her wrist. The kiss had been . . . well, it had been an aberration, that's all. Just an aberration.

"What does anybody need money for?" she asked, getting back to the business at hand.

Considering her question very carefully, he reached up and absently ran a hand through his hair, pushing the shaggy mane into a golden arc. "I don't know. I get along fine without it . . . or I used to."

Stevie watched the beginnings of confusion settle over his face, furrowing his brow and turning his smile into a half-cocked grin.

She screwed the lid on the bottle for the last time, and put it on the shelf. He'd had only one shot and two glasses of beer, but if he drank any more she'd be carrying him out.

"You must have had at least sixty grand when you bought your cabin and acreage," she said, leaning back against the beer cooler and watching him with an amused gaze, a potentially mesmerizing endeavor but one she now felt she could control—until she saw the dreamy softening of his eyes and heard his low, sexy chuckle.

"Well that was a helluva piece of luck in Vegas, at the outdoor trade show back in eighty . . . eighty . . . a few years back. I didn't find a sponsor, but I ended up with plenty of money anyway. Do you play poker?" His eyes refocused for a moment. At the negative shake of her head, he let out a heavy sigh and drifted back toward oblivion.

"Too bad, 'cause I don't have the money now. It's gone, alluvit." Damn, he was tired, he realized.

Against every polite and grateful bone in her body, Stevie's easy smile blossomed into a full-blown grin. Nola had been right, she silently conceded, Halsey Morgan was broke. But before that, he'd been lucky, she thought with more than a fair share of skepticism. She'd never heard of anybody winning that kind of money at poker.

"Well, that's too bad, Hal. Why don't we head home?"

"What about him?" He pointed toward the hall, and his arm kept going, sliding all the way across the bar until his face dropped flat against the polished oak. A swath of flaxen hair fell over his forehead.

Stevie stared at the silky veil covering his face, silently fighting the temptation to reach over and brush it back behind his ears. It would be so easy. He wouldn't even know.

"Don't you worry about old Kong," she said quickly. "I'll call my brother. He'll come and pick him up."

"That's shnice." He felt a little woozy too. Maybe he could hit her up for a sandwich or something . . . something. There had been something he wanted from her. He rolled his head sideways, his eyes drifting up the full length of her legs and over the curve of her hips to the great curve of her breasts. No, he slowly decided, he didn't think he could get that, not all of it, not yet.

"That's what the sheriff is for, to do nice things." Stevie pushed herself off the cooler and stepped into the hall. If she smiled any wider, her face was going to bust.

A moment on the phone took care of Kong Kingman. Gene had his own key, so they didn't have to wait. Stevie strolled back around the end of the bar and kindly helped Hal to his feet.

"What did you shay you needed my money for?" he asked, draping his arm over her shoulders and getting it all tangled up in a silky expanse of honey-colored hair.

"To get out of this dumpy little piece of paradise . . . and maybe go on safari," she added thoughtfully, rearranging his arm and flicking off the lights before opening the door. "Or maybe I'll follow in the footsteps of the great Halsey Morgan and island-hop the South Pacific. What do you think?" Teasing gray eyes looked up at him from under thick, dark lashes.

Hal thought it sounded like a damned good idea, a real bang-up damned good idea—especially if she invited him to go along. Hell, he'd practically invented safari, and, geez, what he didn't know about the South Pacific—well, hell, he knew it all. And when they got tired of sun-washed beaches and swaying palm trees, maybe she'd like to go to Alaska, or . . . what was the name of that little country where they had all the big mountains? The one where he'd almost frozen to death the time he'd . . .

Three

She'd drunk him under the table.

Hal let out with a heavy moan and rolled over in the bed, right into something big and solid and alive.

"Damn," he said softly. Somehow he'd gotten lucky the night before, and he didn't remember a minute of it. Chalking his fortune, or misfortune, up to fate, he tried to slip back into unconsciousness. Maybe with a little more sleep the memories would come back. He and the silky-haired, long-legged goddess must have made magic.

A low, rumbling, and distinctly nonfeminine groan forced his eyes open to a narrow slit. Then something wet and distinctly nonhuman slicked up the back of his neck and behind his ear. Hal squeezed his eyes shut and pulled the pillow over his head. He wasn't ready for this—whatever it was.

His bedmate had other ideas, though. More groans, grunts, and an inordinate amount of shuffling around gave him no choice but to drag the pillow off his head and check things out.

Too close for comfort, the biggest, softest eyes in the world, one blue and one brown, gazed at him from the other pillow with a fondness Hal knew he didn't deserve. The tongue slid out again and left a wet trail up his cheek.

"What's your name, huh?" Despite the bongo beat in his head, a weak smile touched the corner of his mouth. He reached out to scratch his new friend behind the ear. The husky groaned again in pleasure, tail thumping. Hal ran his fingers through the thick soft fur, following a red collar down to a blue tag. It said "Tiva" on one side and "Stevie Lee Brown, Trail's End Bar, Grand Lake, Colorado" on the other. The pounding behind his temples picked up in rhythm, and Hal swore softly, rolling over and burying his head back into the pillow. The lady had shown him no mercy last night—and obviously little else.

Not surprising, her husky seemed like-minded. The dog hopped off the bed and walked over to the door, where she whined and scratched until he finally dragged himself to his feet. With his eyes barely open, Hal shuffled across the cabin, bitching and moaning all the way. He really needed a cup of coffee. He really needed something to eat.

Damn! His groceries! As if on cue, he stumbled into a box on the kitchen floor, stubbing his toe and giving himself a new pain to worry over.

Okay, he thought, leaning back on the table and holding his aching head in his hand, so the lady wasn't all bad. She'd gotten him home, gotten his groceries home, and set him up with a warm girl named Tiva to keep him from freezing.

Another moment of standing there made him

realize something else. She'd also stoked up his old wood stove. Was there no end to the lady's good deeds? A particularly painful sequence of throbs convinced him otherwise. She wouldn't get any gold-plated references from him. But as long as she had the stove going, he might as well start some coffee brewing. Maybe a gallon or two would clear the fuzziness from his brain.

Still holding his head, he moved to the sink, turned on the tap, and immediately felt like an idiot. Of course, nothing came out. When he'd left for his tropical sojourn, he'd closed the cabin up tight, which included draining the pipes and having the power turned off. Sometimes he wished he wasn't so thorough.

A sharp bark from the husky startled him into a painful jerk. Right, he thought wearily, let the dog out. He took two more steps forward, opened the door, and was blasted in the face with pure Rocky Mountain sunshine, a hundred volts of it. His eyes snapped closed so fast and with such force that for a second, Hal was afraid he might not ever get them open. No such luck.

Squinting through a tiny slit, he forced himself outside, one arm raised in front of his face. Yessiree, the Rockies were beauties all right. Young and majestic, they jutted into a cornflower-blue sky scudded with clouds, one hundred and eighty degrees of Continental Divide stretching across the horizon. A rolling, wildflower meadow sloped down from his cabin to a forest of lodgepole pines. Facing to the south, it was almost bare of snow. Even through his pain, he appreciated the pastoral scene, and for the first time was glad he'd come home.

The realization carried him off the front porch

and into knee-high grass and sage. It helped him lower his arm and take a good look around. His gaze tracked the edge of the meadow, down one side and up the other, to a two-story, A-frame sitting at the top. He knew right away it was Stevie Lee Brown's—and suddenly his thoughts weren't quite so bucolic.

Considering all the trouble she'd gotten him into the previous night, he figured she still owed him. A cup of coffee and a hot shower were a good place for her to start, but it was only a start. By the time he'd organized a clean set of clothes and his toothbrush, he'd tacked a couple more requests onto his list, favors he'd meant to ask, the very vital innards of his plan for getting out of his financial mess, and closer to sweet Stevie Lee. The lady hadn't seen the last of him, not by a long shot.

Stevie nursed her third cup of coffee—mud, her father called it—and continued pushing the numbers this way and that on the profit and loss statement. Kip 'TNT' Brown hadn't done her any favors when he'd left her the bar to run in their divorce settlement. The equity she still owed him was a major part of her debt problem. She needed a helluva summer, or she and the Trail's End would really come to the end of their trails. A look at the numbers told her it would take something more along the lines of a miracle for her to scrape together the third installment of Hal Morgan's taxes.

Perversely, the thought brought a small, private smile to her face. Toying with her cup, she let her gaze drift out the window to the pine-forested

ridge behind her cabin. *Halsey Morgan was alive.*
Or at least he had been when she'd finally gotten
him into bed.

The memory of his kiss and of his entreaties for
her to join him in his antique four-poster brought
a soft blush to her cheeks. The man sure had a
sweet streak in him when he wanted something.
In languages she'd never even heard before, let
alone understood, he'd whispered his sensual
promises in her ear.

She lifted her hand and absently ran it through
the loose tendrils of hair tickling her cheek, unconsciously recalling the softness of his mouth
against her skin, the rough timbre of his voice—
and her blush deepened. Maybe she had understood his words better than she'd let on. Why else
would she have threatened to drop him in the
snow if he didn't stop talking?

Foolishness, her common sense warned, pure
foolishness. She had enough problems without
allowing a mere physical attraction to mess up
her life. He might look like a Nordic god, but he
was trouble with a capital T, and worse, he was a
traveling man. She had decided a long time ago
that the next time somebody wandered off into
the world, it was going to be Stevie Lee Brown,
not some man with her heart in the palm of his
hand.

"Well, that settles that," she whispered to herself quite convincingly and forced her attention
back to her books.

Tired of looking at net losses, she searched
through her papers for her balance sheet full of
liabilities. She picked the form out of the sloppy
pile, and a red pen rolled off and leaked on her

blue-and-white checkered tablecloth. *Typical,* she thought. She was floating in red ink.

Last week, she'd offered Jake, the hottest bartender in town, double his wage at The Emporium, and he'd turned her down. Maybe a stock option was in order. Sure, she thought, that was what Jake wanted—stock in a broken-down bar. She took another sip of coffee and rearranged the numbers on her balance sheet, reversing the debits and credits just for kicks.

If she didn't have a bartender, a darn good bartender, by the next weekend, she might as well close her doors. She and her brother Doug would never be able to pump enough business through the Trail, not without killing themselves. And death, she was sure, was not on the top of Doug's priority list for the summer.

Young and in love, she knew he planned on having his nights free and two days off a week. Her mother had offered to help out, but sweet as the offer was, Stevie doubted if her scatterbrained mom could take the pressure. No, what she needed was someone to charm the crowds away from Jake Stone at The Emporium. She needed a good-looking, fast-talking—

A knock on the door interrupted her thoughts.

"Come in," she hollered, reaching across the table and flipping off the lock. The door opened but no one came in, and Stevie glanced up.

If she'd had a cat, it could have dragged him in.

"Good morning." She deliberately added a bright sparkle to her voice, and watched him carefully, gauging his hangover by the depth of his wince. There was a slight crinkle to the eyes, his mouth was holding firm—he wasn't in too bad of shape, she decided.

"Nice try, Stevie. What did you do? Mickey Finn me?" Sarcasm, pure and simple, and thicker than molasses, rolled off his lips and right off her back. She wasn't going to let him get around her defenses again.

"If I had, you wouldn't know it yet." One sable brow arched above her clear gray eyes. "You should have told me you couldn't hold your liquor. I do keep a full stock of soft drinks."

Two very bloodshot, indigo-blue eyes narrowed at her from beneath a Dodgers cap. The white-blond hair sticking out on either side of his hat reminded her of fairy wings, but she doubted if he wanted to hear about it. She also doubted if he wanted to know that he'd forgotten to zip his pants.

"Funny how I never had that problem before." His voice, rough and gravelly the night before, was positively jagged this morning.

"The altitude does crazy things to a person sometimes," she said, leaning back in her chair and rocking it on two legs. "Makes them dizzy, lowers their tolerance for alcohol, maybe freezes them to death in their sleep"—she not so subtly hinted at all the work she'd done last night—"I'm glad to see you didn't have that problem."

"Guess your luck finally ran out." Try as he might, he was having a hard time holding onto his anger.

"It's not the first time," she confessed with an unperturbed smile. "Probably won't be the last."

Well, he thought, she sure hadn't lost any of her chutzpah, and she was even prettier than he'd remembered. The upturned collar on her white sweater framed a face he'd seen more than once in his dreams. It was strange that delicate never crossed his mind, he thought as he looked at the clean, gently curved angles of her brow and cheeks, the bare hint of freckles across the bridge of her nose, or the full softness of her lips. Kissing came to mind, lots of it. With very little effort, he remembered the taste of her on his tongue, the feel of her in his hands and under his mouth.

"How are *you* feeling this morning?" he asked, keeping his thoughts to himself, and, hopefully, the leering gleam out of his eyes.

"Better than you look," Stevie lied, enjoying the easy banter, and despite her best intentions, the scenery. Even hung over, he looked good, real good. The muscles in his arms, though relaxed, were tight and fully curved, hard and nut-brown against the whiteness of a color-splashed T-shirt, which she was happy to see covered his open fly. Underneath the cotton, she saw the ripple of even more clean muscle as he shifted his body and rested against the doorjamb. Then, of course, there was the dark stretch of bare skin revealed by the thigh-length tear in his soft denim jeans. Therein stood the pleasure and the trouble in looking at him.

But Kip had taught her a lesson about good-looking men. She refused to make the same mistake twice, and therein stood her protection against Hal's incredibly blue eyes. As long as she didn't linger, as long as she kept the conversation going, she was immune—at least for all practical purposes. Last night's moments of sensual confusion were history.

"That's not saying a helluva lot." The lift of his eyebrows told her he expected more.

Graciously, she conceded. "Okay, thanks to you and your chivalry, I'm feeling pretty good."

Finally, some gratitude; he felt better already.

"For a cup of coffee, I'll go back into town and break his arms, or his legs, or his neck. Your choice. Throw in a hot shower, and I'll break every bone in his body," Hal said kiddingly.

She'd already figured out that Halsey Morgan wasn't a man who gave up easily. She also hadn't expected to get off with a few beers and a shot of scotch, especially since they'd done him more harm than good.

"Coffee's on the house," she said, dropping her chair back to four legs and rising. "But I'll warn you, most of the time I can't give it away. My dad won't get within ten feet of the stuff."

"I think I can handle it," he replied, stepping in out of the sunshine and into the warmth of the kitchen.

Passing him on her way to the counter, Stevie tossed her braid over her shoulder and said, "We'll see."

The indication, however slight, was enough to form a doubt in his mind. He'd never been cut down by a cup of coffee before, but if it could possibly happen, he knew it would be hers that did it to him.

While he settled into a chair, Stevie busied herself with finding an unchipped mug. The task almost proved beyond her as she passed over first one and then another, until she saw a black and white one in the far corner of the cupboard, her "Don't bother me, I'm having a mid-life crisis" mug. The phrase matched Hal Morgan's morning to a tee, and smothering a chuckle, she filled it.

Passing him the cup first, she rested back against the counter and waited.

Hal didn't like the way she was looking at him, but he forged ahead, passing the coffee under his nose. "Smells great," he said, somewhat surprised. He glanced down. "Looks good." Then he saw the inscription. "Cute cup," he finished off with a tight smile and lifted the mug to his mouth.

"It was a gift from a friend"—Stevie casually crossed her arms—"to celebrate my divorce."

Hal choked on her words and the god-awful brew. Sputtering and mad, he leveled a steely-eyed glare at her. "Dammit, Stevie, you did that on purpose! You knew I was coming and you set me up!"

Wide, innocent eyes met his. "I'm divorced," she said defensively.

That was shock enough in itself, but Hal wasn't about to admit it. "You know what I mean. Nobody would drink that . . . that claptrap."

"Claptrap?"

"Claptrap," he repeated more forcefully, in lieu of a truer description. "You come down to my place tomorrow, and I'll teach you how to make a cup of coffee, real coffee. Hell, I've done better in a blizzard with a tin can."

"Well you can just take your tin can and do it again," she said, pushing off the counter and whisking the mug out of his hand.

"I guess I'm going to have to. Can I have my shower first."

"What's the matter? Is there a water shortage in the meadow I don't know about?"

"I don't have any power, and no power means no pump, and no pump means no water"—he lifted his cap and smoothed his hair back underneath—"Basic physics."

Slanting him a dry look, she called his bluff. "You don't know anything about physics."

Hal didn't miss the slight questioning tone of

her words, and a slow, teasing grin curved his mouth. "No," he admitted. "But I figured you didn't either." He had her there, his first victory. Lord, it felt good.

Stevie felt her advantage and her confidence slip. "Since when did I become your guardian angel?"

"Since I became yours." He was on a roll.

"You only had to hit him once."

"Oh, no, Stevie. You've got it backwards." If possible, his grin broadened. "*Only once* was enough."

Men, she thought with a sigh, putting her hand on her hip and watching his smile get cockier by the second. She owed him, he knew it, and he wasn't about to let her forget it. Reluctantly she nodded toward the rest of the cabin. "The bathroom is on the left. You can't miss it."

Whistling a tuneless tune, Hal moseyed out of the kitchen and gave himself the grand tour on the way to the bathroom. The rest of her home was small but nice, like her kitchen. A big picture window in her living room gave her the same spectacular view he had from his front porch. Except she could cozy up in front of her stone fireplace and enjoy it, whereas he had to either go outside, or prop himself up in bed.

Her furniture wasn't like most that could be found in a mountain cabin. It certainly wasn't anything like his; hers matched. Two navy-blue chairs with beige stripes flanked a solid navy-blue sofa. A baby-blue and white rag rug covered the floor between the set. On the opposite wall from the fireplace, a set of built-in shelves overflowed with books and magazines. He'd only had two books on the island with him: *Remembrance of*

Things Past—a bon voyage gift from a friend for those long nights on the ocean alone—and a Travis McGee novel. He'd almost memorized the McGee book.

Curiosity propelled him toward the shelves, where it took him all of thirty seconds to discern her reading interests. Tahiti, Nepal, West Africa, the names crossed his mind like old friends.

"*Beyond the High Himalayas; Lost Cities of China, Central Asia, and India; Dollarwise Guide to the Caribbean,*" he whispered the titles as his finger ran along the spines. He shifted his gaze, passing over a shelf filled with *National Geographic* magazines, to the one crammed full of travel brochures hawking their wares—Tent Safaries, Adventure Trekking, Balloon Tours of Kenyan Game Reserves. The glossy pages fell from his fingertips one after the other, gradually bringing a memory to the surface—"*. . . on safari, or island-hop the South Pacific.*"—and another piece of his plan clicked into place. He had her where he wanted her, right in the palm of his hand.

Grinning with confidence, Hal strode into the bathroom and came to a sudden halt. Hanging from an inside clothesline was the most wonderful stuff—pale yellow with lace, bright blue without, creamy silk, and soft pink, one-piece, and two-piece and all the in-between stuff. The bathroom looked like an erotic gypsy carnival.

He thought back to Stevie Lee, standing in the kitchen in her hiking boots, faded jeans, and bulky sweater—and Lord knew what else—and another stream of muttered curses floated from his lips. All he'd wanted was a cup of coffee and a hot shower, and now she'd ruined them both.

Still cussing, he reached for the cold water tap.

• • •

Stevie turned the steaks over and shoved them back under the broiler. Hash browns and eggs sizzled in a frying pan on top of the stove.

"That was quick." She glanced up when Hal returned. Then she took another look, and felt her heart simultaneously rise to her throat and drop into the pit of her stomach—an incredibly disconcerting experience.

A hung over, slightly rumpled, good-looking man had walked out of her kitchen. A sun-god had returned in his place.

A soft white, collarless shirt clung to his damp skin, caressing the solid curves of his chest and arms. Baggy, black cotton pants hung dangerously low around his hips, and put a hundred sensual images in her mind. Clean-shaven with his hair wet and slicked back, his face did the same—images of her mouth trailing across his golden skin, of her fingers tangling through his flaxen hair and curling around the back of his neck ran rampant in her head.

"Looks as if you've got enough food there to feed an army, Stevie. I thought all women watched their weight." He spoke to her, but thankfully his eyes remained locked on the frying pan, giving her a moment to compose herself. It wasn't long enough, but she did her best.

"Don't worry. Most of it's yours. I thought I'd . . . uh . . . get all of this gratitude business out of the way in one fell swoop." She'd also thought about Nola's recital of his grocery list, and of her freezer full of prime Colorado beef. She'd forgotten about the special intimacy implied in sharing breakfast.

"You're just full of good ideas, aren't you?" he

looked up with a mischievous light warming the depths of his eyes.

She was full of ideas all right, tempting, seductive ideas. They whirled around her imagination and teased her body with memories of the previous night. Ideas involving two people and little else.

"What did you eat when you were shipwrecked?" she asked, rushing into the moment of silence, clamping down on her capricious thoughts.

"Raw fish."

"How interesting." Good Lord, even his voice had taken on a sexual undertone. "Raw, yes, that's quite interesting."

"My matches got wet." He chuckled. "I'm a regular sushi chef."

"Well, yes, I'd guess so. We don't get much call for sushi in Grand Lake. Actually, I don't think we've ever had a sushi chef in town." She was babbling and staring, and she had to stop both. "Do you want milk or juice?" Finally, a coherent statement. She latched onto the moment of lucidity, turning away from him and going to the cupboard for plates.

Hal's gaze followed her across the room, lingering on the sway of her hips and the curve of her waist. He wanted to know what she was wearing underneath her sweater and her jeans. He wanted to know what erotic delicacy slid against her skin, but he said, "Milk."

"Go ahead and sit down. It's ready."

He did as he was told, which was a nice change, and Stevie served up breakfast. The minute her bottom hit the chair, she dug in, wanting to get it over with. Lost in her own disconcerted thoughts, she made all the little clattering noises with her knife and fork people usually make when they eat but usually nobody notices—unless the nobody is praying over his food.

"Excuse me. I didn't think about saying grace." She whispered a hushed apology and belatedly closed her eyes.

"It's a habit I picked up on the island. Every time I caught a fish, I fell to my knees and yelled "Thank God!" his voice rose to a crescendo, popping her eyes open.

"Well, yes, I can understand that, of course." *Was he nuts?*

"Naturally, I've toned it down a bit for civilization."

"Naturally." Stevie discreetly rolled her eyes and went back to eating her breakfast, hoping they wouldn't have any more outbursts, praying that he'd eat and leave, and that she'd be done with him.

Hungry guests a happy hostess makes, Stevie silently repeated her mother's favorite phrase for the third time, once for each piece of toast he'd eaten after he'd finished off ten ounces of rib eye steak, half a pound of hash browns, and two eggs. He was never going to leave, she just knew it. But she wasn't nearly as concerned as she'd been. There was something about watching a marathon eating spree that wore the nervous, sexual energy right out of her.

Resting her elbows on the table and her head in her hands, she watched him devour another slice of toast, and wondered what she'd feed him next. Her half-gallon carton of milk registered empty. Only a heel of bread remained in the wrapper.

"You should have warned me about your hollow leg."

Completely nonplussed by her barb, he glanced up and grinned. "A guy can store up a lot of hunger living on raw fish."

"No kidding," she said dryly, settling back in her chair and waiting for him to pounce on the last piece of bread. She didn't have to wait long.

As he leaned forward to put it in the toaster, she spied a telltale dent in his ear, and a smile twitched the corner of her mouth. No doubt about it, Hal Morgan was full of surprises.

"What happened to your earring?" she asked, mildly intrigued.

"I had to pawn my diamond in Oahu. Do you want to go halfsies on the toast?"

She shook her head and leaned in closer. "You had a *diamond* earring?"

"What I had was a diamond. I figured the safest place for it was in my ear. Turned out to be a real good idea."

Definitely intrigued, Stevie had to ask, "What do you mean, best place for it?"

"When *Freedom*, my sailboat, crashed on the island, a lot of my stuff disappeared. But my good luck charm"—he reached up and tugged his ear, grinning—"she was safe and sound."

"Good luck charm?" her tone cast serious doubt on his terminology. "You end up shipwrecked on a deserted tropical island—and you've still got a 'good luck charm?' Where did you get such a great piece of luck?"

"I picked it up the hard way . . . running for my life on a beach in South Africa." The toast popped up, and he slathered it with butter and jam.

Sighing, she rested her head on the table and

gave him a choice. "Do you want to tell me about it? Or do you want me to drag it out of you?"

He took a bite of toast and chewed it thoughtfully for a moment. "I guess that all depends, Stevie. Are we talking a real physical dragging out? With you and me rolling around on the floor and—"

"Don't press your luck," she interrupted, cautioning him with a lift of her brow.

Teasing blue eyes flashed at her from across the table. "I'd been in Angola for a few weeks," he started in. "Things were heating up with the government and the guerillas, and it was time to get out." Slowly but surely, his eyes took on a faraway look. "When this small freighter came through looking for crew, I signed on as far as South Africa. I knew a couple of guys there, and I figured we could work a deal to get me back to Australia—I've got lots of friends in Australia," he said pointedly, and Stevie wondered why, but she didn't interrupt him. "Anyway, about a week out, I got to thinking that this little tramp wasn't all she'd been cracked up to be. It doesn't take an expert to know when you're going around in circles, even in the middle of the ocean. Sure enough, one night the captain hits me up for 'shore duty.' I figured he was picking up contraband, maybe running guns back to Angola. It turned out to be a lot less organized and a lot more dangerous than gunrunning." He stopped to take another bite of toast.

Hanging off the edge of her chair, Stevie waited for him to continue, and waited. "Well?" she finally prompted, not even trying to disguise her burning curiosity.

"Well . . . he had this crazy scheme concerning

the diamond business. 'There for the picking,' he said. 'Just laying in the sand.' 'No,' I said. He pulled a gun—and I got in the boat."

"And?"

"And sure enough, they were just laying in the sand, right along with about a dozen armed guards and Lord knows how many Dobermans. Lord, I hate Dobermans."

"You stole a diamond?" Her eyes widened even further.

"Actually, it was pretty fair trade. The dogs got a piece of my backside, and I got two carats of uncut stone. Do you want to see my scars?"

Stevie sat back in her chair, slack-jawed. She was tempted to say yes, just to make him prove his outlandish story. But he was Halsey Morgan, and she'd heard wilder tales about him.

"I'd say that made for a pretty good piece of luck. What do you think?"

"I think you're crazy," she said honestly.

"I like to think of it as adventurous." A definite gleam sparkled in the depths of his eyes.

"And you can call a grizzly tame, but it don't make it so," she said, still not sure if he'd been pulling her leg.

Ignoring her skepticism, he pushed his empty plate away and relaxed back in his chair. "Well." He sighed, stretching his legs out. "That'll probably kill me."

"Don't you even dare think it," she said in a low voice.

"Just teasing, Stevie. Actually, you've taken real good care of me this morning."

"Then we're even?" One sable brow arched hopefully.

"Not quite, not yet. I think I owe you a little something for your hospitality." He paused for a moment, gearing up for his slam-bang surprise. "How would you like an all-expenses-paid vacation to Australia?"

"Can I leave tonight?" she asked without missing a beat. We'll see who's fooling who, she thought. Then her eyes narrowed to a discerning angle. "Or do you want something first?"

Her ready answer, and her quick summation of the situation, left him speechless.

"Right," she drew the word out on a long breath. "That's what I figured. What is it? Money? Well, I don't have any. No"—she stopped him with a raised hand when he started to explain—"let me guess. Now what have I got that the world-wandering Hal Morgan can't get anyplace else?"

"Besides that." She dismissed his immediate, rakish leer with a flick of her wrist. Emotionally, it took a little more effort. Okay, a lot more effort, she silently conceded to the mocking voice inside her head. The man did have great eyes, and when he turned them on with a smile, she wasn't immune.

She mulled over the other options, and came up with the truth. Leveling her gaze, she said slowly, so he wouldn't miss a word, "Forget it. I'm not hiring you."

"I'm a helluva bartender," he replied in a deeply persuasive drawl, lying through his teeth. At best he figured he'd done enough drinking to make him an expert; from Borneo to Timbuktu, he'd drunk stuff she probably hadn't even heard of. At worst he figured he could fake it.

"Why don't you just ask me to slit my throat and get it over with?" Both of her eyebrows rose this time, adding emphasis to her question. "All that's standing between me and your property is a couple of grand in back taxes. If I give you a job, you'll make that before the Fourth of July." She conveniently left out the part about needing a miracle to stay afloat, let alone pay his taxes.

"A guy's got to eat too."

"Hah!" She gestured at the array of dirty dishes in front of him. "Tell me about it!"

He decided to appeal to her sense of logic. "Stevie"—he leaned forward, resting his hands on the table in a show of honesty recognized all over the world—"I'll get a job whether you hire me or not. Since you have the most to lose, I thought I'd offer my services to you first." Sometimes Hal amazed himself with the line of bull he could concoct out of nothing. "And I was serious about the Australian trip. If you'd like to go someplace else, just say so. I have connections all over the world, and most of them owe me." That part was pure fact. She'd have to search pretty damn hard to find a spot on the map where he didn't know somebody with strings to pull.

He'd answered a number of questions with his soliloquy, and hit them all dead center. The bit about offering services was weak, but then he thought she could pay his taxes again without blinking an eye. She knew it would have been a fight to the finish. Her scrambling to pay her bills and still put some extra aside. And the Australian trip—if anyone else had made the proposal, she would have laughed them out of the kitchen. But his story, completely true or not, had confirmed what she already knew about men like Halsey Morgan. They lived off the grace of the gods and a long and loyal network of friends, where money never changed hands but favors did.

Stevie leaned back in her chair and gave him a critical once-over. She'd hired a few people in her time, and not one of them had hit her with a come-on like his, or a smile like the one he was using to charm her socks off. For a fleeting moment, she wondered how much that smile could mean to her in dollars and cents. Then she wondered for another, and another, while she took in the sensual angles of his face, the hard line of his jaw, the wind-blown look of his hair, and finally she came to a conclusion: He was pure bar bait if she'd ever seen it. She could easily imagine the hordes of women coming to flirt with him, the corresponding hordes of men coming to pick up the women—and all of them glued to their bar stools by his wild stories. It was a hard image to let go of, and that left her with only two problems.

"What's to keep you from paying off the taxes and running out on me midseason? Probably to Australia," she voiced the lesser concern.

"They call it risk, Stevie Lee. How much are you willing to risk on a handshake and a chance to get out of here?"

Coming from the biggest risk taker of them all, his words held a challenge, and a dare. She thought again of another year trapped in Grand Lake, looking at the same old pine-covered mountains. She thought of other mountains, mountains with forests of rhododendrons and cedar, and her own adventuresome spirit rebelled. Then she thought of her second problem—herself.

Twice she'd fallen prey to his blue eyes and golden good looks. Twice he'd effortlessly confused her with his special brand of sensuality. And twice she'd bounced back. Could she keep doing it? Or better yet, could she avoid it all together?

One look told her the latter was asking too much. She might be hardened against love, but she wasn't blind. But then love was different from, well, sex, she thought.

Love was definitely different from sex, and she'd never had one without the other—at least on her side of the bed. Kip had lived by a separate set of rules, or maybe he'd been in love with everybody at the same time. Who knew? And who cared?

You're straying from the point, Stevie. A little voice in the back of her mind gently reminded her of the business at hand. Right, she thought, where was she? Love, sex, and Halsey Morgan.

No! The voice screamed, an alarm went off, and Stevie jumped in her chair.

Hal lurched back in his. Sweet Allah! All he'd asked for was a job. If she thought about it much harder, she was going to blow a fuse.

"Friday, four o'clock." She didn't give herself a chance to change her mind, because above all, she couldn't afford not to hire him. "Saturday will be twelve hours. Sunday and Monday another twelve apiece. It's Memorial Day. You'll 'bar back' this weekend, and we'll split tips. Okay?"

"Okay." Hal grinned in appreciation. The lady did know how to make a decision, and he liked that in a woman, and in a friend. He didn't know what "bar back" meant, but he was sure he could handle anything she threw at him. Anything, he silently reaffirmed, in case his luck changed.

"I'll tell you right now, the day shifts are taken," she continued. "One of my brothers will be coming home from college. He's got a girlfriend, so he likes his nights free. Is that a problem for you?"

"My love life has been pretty weak lately," he confessed with another one of his hundred-dollar smiles.

"Fine." Stevie kept her voice strictly business. She could have told him he'd have his pick of the litter when the ladies of Grand Lake got a look at him, but she didn't. "I pay five bucks an hour plus tips. I don't pay overtime, so if you're going to run to the labor board, tell me now and I'll get somebody else."

"No running. I promise."

Stevie accepted his word without a second thought. She knew he wasn't the type to expect the government or anybody else to solve his problems. She'd only told him to lead up to the trickier condition of his employment.

"Well, that's fine then"—she lowered her gaze, sent up a small prayer, and forged ahead—"there's just . . . uh . . . one other thing—about last night. No kissing."

"No kissing?"

Hazarding a quick glance at him, Stevie nodded.

"You mean like no kissing between you and me?"

Another tilt of her head confirmed his description of the situation.

With effort, Hal kept himself from laughing out loud. His cool little cucumber wasn't so cool after all. He already knew he was going to lie, but he took his time, leaning back in his chair and watching a faint pinkness steal up the creamy curves of her cheeks. Her hands were clasped together in her lap. Her eyes were glued to an unknown spot on the table.

Keeping a straight face and a sincere tone, he agreed to her impossible condition. "Sure, Stevie.

I can see where we could cause a lot of trouble for ourselves if we were always sneaking around kissing. You and me, necking in the back room, lingering long after the customers left. Yes. Yes, I can see that you're right."

Unfortunately Stevie also saw—every single situation he described. But he'd agreed, and that was the important thing. A part of her felt immense relief—and a part of her felt immense disappointment.

Four

Hal shoved his hands into the sudsy water for the millionth time, covering each of the whirring brushes with a highball glass and a collins glass respectively. At least that's what he thought they were. "Bar backing," he discovered, meant dish-pan hands and a lot of running back and forth to the storeroom for more liquor.

Doug, Stevie's brother, piled three more beer mugs onto the tiny space holding too many other dirty glasses, and Hal barely caught a toppled snifter.

"Sorry." The younger man grinned sheepishly. "Good catch, though."

"Thanks." Hal couldn't afford any more bad catches. Immediately after his first miss of the evening, Stevie had called him into the back room and explained her policy on broken glassware—You lose it, you bought it.

"A case of Bud for the cooler," she yelled above the noise as she passed him on the left.

Hal started to move. Doug shoved two more dirty glasses at him and Hal hesitated, wondering if he could make it to the storeroom, unload twenty-four bottles of beer into the refrigerator, and get back before he went broke.

"Gin for the well?" Doug asked, smiling at him from the other end of the bar.

Hal knew he could get the gin. But could he do it without plowing into Stevie again? He eyed the eight feet of distance to the hall where the well liquor was stored, all the time washing glasses as if his life depended on it, trying to get ahead, timing his move to avoid colliding with her as she worked both ends of the bar.

The evening had started out quiet enough, with just a few locals coming in for a beer and a little bit of gossip. But at about eight o'clock the week-enders had arrived, and it had been chaos ever since.

Go! he said to himself. Hal dashed into the hall, grabbed the gin, and returned in time to catch a couple of glasses that were falling into the sink. He knew from experience that every time he lost one in the sink he had to clean out the broken glass or risk turning his hands into hamburger meat. At this point, he didn't have time to clean out the sink.

Washing away, he wondered how Stevie and Doug did it. Like a finely choreographed dance, they worked around each other, mixing drinks and drawing beers while keeping up a steady stream of chatter. On top of all that, they kept the cash register ringing, calling out tabs and making change—but not much change.

The two exerted a very subtle pressure on the customers for tips. Any money coming over the bar was fair game, and if the amount given was close to the amount owed, the change went into a brandy snifter on the shelf behind the bar, no questions asked. The ancient custom of Arabic baksheesh, Chinese squeeze, reached new heights at the Trail's End Bar.

"Damn!" Doug jerked his bloody hand away from a broken beer mug. "Take over, Hal, I'll be back in a minute. Stevie! Band-Aids still in the top drawer?"

"On the left."

Take over? Hal looked up with a sinking feeling. He had to be kidding.

A man edged his way between the customers seated at the bar. "Two gin and tonics."

Hal quickly shoveled ice into the two glasses he'd just pulled out of the rinse water. He set them on the bar and ran his fingers over the bottles in the well, searching for the gin. Faster than he'd dared to hope, he found it. The Trail's End operated without the constraints of a jigger, so he poured away, guessing the amount. A couple of quick shots out of the soda gun and he'd served his first two drinks.

"Five bucks," he said to the man, making another guess.

The man handed him six, his first tip.

"May I have a manhattan, please." A petite blonde sidled up to the bar and graced him with a smile. "You must be new in town." She leaned in closer, revealing an impressive cleavage.

Hal didn't have time for the view. He also didn't have any idea of what went into a manhattan. He glanced toward Stevie, looking for help, but she was working about eight drinks of her own.

"What's in it?" he asked the blonde, using his forearm to wipe a stream of sweat off his brow.

"Oh, I don't know. A splash of this, a splash of that." She laughed and leaned in even closer.

"Can we get another couple of beers here?"

"Ask him if he's got any wine, honey. Any red wine."

"I need an old-fashioned, make it two, and a . . ."

". . . another of the same, barkeep. And put some booze in it this time."

Hal was losing it. He looked to Stevie again, and found her staring at him, strangely and intensely, her gray eyes narrowed almost shut, her mouth pulled into a tight line.

"One manhattan coming up." Doug stepped back in, whipping a glass up on the bar. "We've got the house wine—red, white, or pink. Take your pick. Hey, Mac, if I put any more booze in them, you'll be crawling out of here. Hi, Tim. You and Georgia still drinking the same old-fashioneds. That pegs you for a cheesehead every time." He laughed, hands flying, easily working his way through Hal's disaster.

Before Hal could get back to his suds, Stevie swept by him. "I want to see you in the back room. Now."

Again? he thought wearily. How in the hell was he supposed to meet her in the office without the whole inventory of glassware becoming history, and his night's wages becoming nonexistent. His eyes darted to the side, then behind him to the liquor shelves. An empty space! He grabbed a bunch of glasses and shoved them on the shelf, buying himself a minute. Taking ten more glasses with him, a finger in each, he half-ran through the hall and into the back room.

"Yeah?" He stood in front of her desk, chest heaving. A new rivulet of sweat ran down the side of his face. He used his shoulder to wipe it away, clinking the glasses and almost losing a beer mug.

"A bartender," she began, her voice low and strained. "A helluva bartender, you said."

"Yeah," he said, only half-listening. Most of his attention was focused back at the bar, waiting for the crash.

"This deal was supposed to be based on trust, and one day into it you've already proven how little I can trust you."

Hal squinted at her through yet another stream of sweat. "Could we talk about this later? I've already lost a couple of glasses, and—"

"Five glasses, Hal. You've lost five."

She'd been counting? he thought. "Whatever, if I don't get back out there, Doug is going to get swamped."

"Not likely. *He's* a bartender. I don't know what you are, but a bartender you ain't."

The last thing he needed at this point was a rundown of his abilities or the lack thereof. The whole absurd situation sparked his anger.

"And *that's* no bar out there." He waved his arm behind him, toward the front of the house. "It's a zoo!" A wineglass flew off of his little finger and crashed to the floor.

"Six."

Dammit. Six.

"Zoo?"

"A three-ring circus. We need more help," he said, all the while pushing the glass into a pile with his foot.

"More help? And just where do you propose I put them? Hanging from the ceiling by their feet?"

The lady had a smart mouth—and a damn good point. But he wasn't in any mood to concede. "Then we need to expand."

"Hah! I can't even afford what I've got!" With that, she stomped by him and back into the fray.

Hal's chin slumped to his chest. He wasn't ready. He needed a time-out, a minute to catch his breath and get his bearings. But Stevie Lee didn't pay overtime, and she didn't give regulation breaks. What he really needed to know was what in the hell went into a manhattan and all those other drink orders they'd thrown at him. Cussing under his breath, he marched after her.

A totally demoralizing situation awaited him at the bar. Doug was leaning on the cash register, joking with the customers and casually sipping a beer—and there wasn't a dirty glass anywhere. he'd even gotten to the ones stacked on the liquor shelf.

The younger man grinned when Hal approached. "Are you having fun yet?"

Hal felt a smile tug at his mouth, despite his exhaustion. "I don't dare. She'd probably charge me for that too." The lady was well out of earshot, deep in the crowd with a bar tray piled high with glasses. His glasses, he thought with a surprisingly proprietary attitude.

"She's not all bad, really. She's got a sweet side, or at least she did before Kip ran out on her."

An instant zing of curiosity snapped Hal's gaze up to Doug. "Her ex-husband?" he asked, not at all liking the way it sounded.

Doug shrugged. "Some guys just can't be happy with one woman, I guess. Not me though. See the little redhead in the booth over there?" He pointed to the far side of the bar. "Her name is Francine. She belongs to me. I thought you should know."

Through the thinning crowd, Hal saw the spoken-for Francine. Strawberry-blond curls framed an impish face dusted with freckles. Clear blue eyes sparkled with mischief. Something she said caused her friends to burst out laughing, and Hal figured Doug had his work cut out for him.

So did he. He'd never had trouble impressing a woman before, but then up until a week ago, he'd never met Stevie Lee Brown. He searched the room again, and found her talking with a group of lumberjacks. Her eyes had lost their sparkle hours ago, but her mouth still curved into quick, fleeting smiles as she spoke to her customers. A soft, worn pair of jeans loved every one of her curves, up the slender length of her legs to the slight swell of her hips. At her waist, the Dynamite shirt took over, hugging and outlining her back and the fullness of her breasts. The lady was doing things to him that kept him awake at night, and he needed his sleep.

"The guy must have been crazy," he muttered, more to himself than to Doug, but the younger man answered.

" 'TNT' isn't such a bad guy. He just couldn't settle down."

Hal shot him a quizzical glance. " 'TNT'?" he questioned. He didn't have a sister, but if he had, he sure wouldn't take such a friendly attitude toward a man who'd cheated on her. Once again the thought seemed incomprehensible.

"Yeah, like in dynamite. That's his car Stevie drives. Or it used to be anyway. I guess it belongs to her now."

Dynamite. Against his will, Hal's gaze drifted

back to Stevie and her red shirt, and suddenly it didn't look quite as sexy as he'd thought.

"That Kip." Doug chuckled. "He's something. Really loves a good party. Hell, Kip loves a bad party. He and Stevie sure made the rounds when they were young."

Two things bothered Hal about Doug's reminiscing: The past tense verb in front of "young," and the thought of Stevie "making the rounds" with a groping party animal. He'd heard enough.

But Doug was just getting warmed up. "You should have seen their wedding. It was the biggest thing to hit this county in twenty years. Must have been two hundred people there, practically everybody in town. And the cars"—a wistful note crept into his voice—"Kip knows everybody with a hot car on the Western Slope. It was the first time I ever sat in a Porsche."

Hal recognized a severe case of hero worship when it hit him in the face, but this was the first time he hadn't been the hero. He'd like to see this Kip guy try to climb Everest, or raft the Waghi River. As a matter of fact, he'd like to see it real bad.

"Yep, we all thought Stevie did good for herself when she finally got Kip to the altar. Mom and Dad pitched in with Mr. and Mrs. Brown and built them that cabin for a wedding present, right on the edge of the ranch, right where Stevie wanted it."

The A-frame had been a wedding present? A sick feeling plummeted into the middle of Hal's stomach. Stevie had told him it was only two years old. This wasn't an old ex-husband they were talking about. This was a brand new ex-husband.

"Kip spoiled her, too, even at the divorce. He let her have the house and the car and half interest in this place. If Stevie hadn't caught him red-handed, they'd probably still be together."

Thankfully, a man came up to order a drink, distracting Doug from the conversation. But Hal wasn't any happier left alone with his thoughts.

A jerk named TNT, who fancied himself hot as dynamite had loved, spoiled, and walked out on a woman who treated Hal like a bad case of hives, something to be endured. Hal couldn't figure it: he wasn't such a bad guy. But then again, every car he'd ever owned bore a remarkable resemblance, in looks and temperament, to his truck. The only house he'd ever owned was almost a memory—and the adventuring business wasn't something you could just up and give to somebody, at least not the way he went about it. Not many people wanted to paddle their guts out on a white-water river for three meals a day and damn little else, or haul a hundred and twenty pound pack up the side of an unforgiving mountain for bragging rights and a few items of equipment.

Hal liked things that way. The fewer people out there cluttering up the wild places, the better. But he liked something else too—the way Stevie Lee made him feel—and he could imagine a thousand ways to spoil her, none of which he could afford. Even with all the facts in place, he wanted her.

Damn. Life was suddenly getting a lot more complicated.

Friday rolled into Saturday, into Sunday, and finally into Monday, seemingly without end. She'd said he'd be working twelve-hour days, but fourteen or sixteen had proven to be the norm. Under

Doug's tutelage, Hal's drink repertoire had risen dramatically. Even more amazing for someone used to having a few hundred miles between himself and the rest of humanity, he'd learned the finer moves of working with two people in a cramped space without stepping on anybody's toes. But he hadn't been able to get Stevie alone for a minute.

Hal stacked the last clean glass on the shelf, then took it back down to wipe a few spots off with his bar towel. He twisted the glass around the cloth and checked out the bar. The coolers were stocked with beer, the place was tidy, and the chaotic crowds had piddled out to a few regulars. It was time to make his move.

Tossing the towel over his shoulder, he called to Doug, "I'm taking a break."

The younger man nodded and went back to counting out their tips on the bar.

". . . four, five, six, seven hundred," Stevie whispered under her breath. "And twenty, forty." Seven hundred and forty dollars. She counted it again.

"Hmm, not bad." She tippity-tapped the number onto her calculator, then picked up a bundle of tens.

Stacks of cardboard boxes, most of them empty, towered over the side of her rolltop desk, blocking the overhead light and throwing her slender form into the slanted shadow of the ceiling fan. Various and sundry pieces of replacement parts, tools, and busted equipment littered the remaining floor space.

Standing in the doorway, Hal looked at the mess and wondered how she ever got any work done. Her desk reminded him of a miniature junkyard.

Empty beer bottles and pop cans were scattered here and there like beacons among the flat paper waste.

'For double wages, I'll clean this place up for you," he offered from across the infamous back room.

Stevie swivelled her chair around, one pencil in her hand, another stuck behind her ear. "Don't even try it, mister. I've got a system going here." A surprisingly soft smile curved her full, wide mouth, sending a jolt of anticipation through his chest. Then she went and ruined it. "This is the best Memorial Day weekend the Trail's ever done, close to thirty-five hundred dollars."

"Looks as though I'm earning my keep," he said dryly. Was money all she ever thought about? he wondered.

She answered him silently with an arched brow, and swivelled herself around and went back to work.

"What's the big deal, anyway," he continued, leaning his shoulder against the door frame. "According to Doug, good old Kip set you up for life."

"If you call ridiculous car payments, an outrageous mortgage, and a piece of a decrepit bar that can't even pay for the beer being set up for life, then he did." While she talked, she shuffled through the piles of ledgers and papers on the desk, eventually coming up with a rubber band. "Frankly, I had something else in mind."

Her words, however lightly spoken, caused an uneasy tightening in his chest.

"Thought you were smarter than that, Stevie Lee," he said softly, hurting for her and not knowing exactly why. Sure, he'd seen how hard she worked, keeping a lid on the pandemonium and charming the customers. But he'd also seen her drop with exhaustion at the end of each night.

From the back, he saw her lift one shoulder in a slight shrug. "It was a small price to pay to get rid of him."

He took her nonchalance as a cue and sure rejection of any pity he might have offered, if he'd been dumb enough to offer Stevie Lee Brown pity. Changing tactics, he said in a lighter tone, "I guess I showed up in the nick of time."

She replied silently again, this time lifting both shoulders in an all-out, dismissive shrug.

Okay, Hal, you've tried the subtle approach.

Stevie sensed his encroaching presence and shifted closer to her calculator, trying with all her heart to ignore him, wishing he'd get what he'd come for and leave. Then she felt a warm tingle on the back of her neck, and a corresponding heat in her cheeks. Damn him. What did he think he was doing? She dared to look up and immediately wished she hadn't.

The broken shafts of light from the ceiling fan cast him in shadow, adding mystery and danger to a face she'd been secretly memorizing all weekend. His rolled up sleeves and open collar of his shirt revealed a warm, dark brown body, lean with muscle and ready for—what? Stevie unconsciously scooted closer to her desk.

Hal was taking his time, enjoying the view, and stalking her, slowly, easily, and inevitably. His gaze traveled up the length of her legs to the wide leather belt cinching her waist. A white T-shirt, he'd like to see wet, clung to her upper body.

"Thanks for not firing me Friday night." He lifted two of the reinforced cardboard boxes off the stack and dropped them on the near side of her desk, neatly trapping her between himself and the wall.

Stevie's eyes widened as he sat down on the double box, knees splayed, booted feet planted firmly on the floor. A tiny, delayed shot of panic released in her brain. "You're welcome. You'll . . . um . . . get the hang of it."

'Yeah, I think I will." Hal made himself comfortable and watched her, letting his anticipation build. He'd waited a long time. "Is it going to be crazy like that every weekend?"

"No. We'll get hit again on the Fourth, and Labor Day weekend, but the rest of the time it will just be busy, not cra—What are you doing?"

With the toe of his boot, Hal swivelled her chair around, putting her between his legs. Her tiny shot of panic turned into a heart-pounding wave.

"Hal," she said with a gasp, pressing back into the chair. Her braid slid over her shoulder, making a honey-colored ribbon down the front of her shirt. "Wha-what do you think you're doing?"

"Well, Stevie, I'll tell you," he said in a soft drawl, leaning in close and resting his hands on the arms of the chair. "For a week and a half all I've been able to think about is kissing you again. . . ."

The rolling roughness of his voice pulled her ever-widening eyes up to meet the indigo sultriness of his.

"Hal, you promised." Slight desperation made her voice weak, and, oh, so vulnerable to the power of his.

". . . But I'm having trouble pulling it off." His mouth lowered to her cheek, and his words blew against her skin. "I was hoping you'd help me, maybe we could practice for a while." Every phrase drew him closer to the sweet nape of her neck. At her ear, he paused and whispered, "Come on, Stevie . . . help me." Then his mouth opened.

The warmth, and the wetness, and the wildness of his touch exploded across her skin, drowning reason with desire. He was above her and over her, his hands linking behind her head, gently nudging her, coaxing her, asking her to turn her mouth into his.

"Hal . . ." His name whispered from her lips on a soft moan. "Please, no."

"Shh . . ." His hand came around the side of her face, cupping her chin and making the decision for her.

More lost than she'd ever been, Stevie opened her mouth, and slowly sank into the heat and passion of his kiss. A depthless longing lifted her hands to the bare skin of his arms, just to feel the warmth and the hardness of him. Beneath her fingers, his muscles flexed and tightened, drawing her closer.

Without warning Hal had slipped in over his head. He'd started something he didn't want to end. Sweet, sweet, Stevie Lee surprised him again and again with the hunger of her touch, the lazy track of her tongue in his mouth, the pressure of her knee on the inside of his thigh. A slow ache drew a groan of pleasure from his mouth into hers. He slid his arm behind her back and pulled her out of the chair and between his legs. He needed her closer, wanted her fully against him.

"Don't mind me, kids. I'm just getting a case of beer for the cooler."

Stevie instantly froze in his arms. Hal swore, first in Spanish, then Arabic—the little rat, he thought. The coolers were fully stocked.

Doug hefted the case and walked back toward the hall.

Thoroughly flustered and even more embarrassed, Stevie disentangled herself from his passionate embrace.

"Stevie," he began.

"No. No, Hal. I can't afford this . . . this situation. You, me, I can't afford this." She turned away, but Hal caught her hand and pulled her back into his arms. Lowering his mouth to hers, he reminded her of what they'd shared. Once again she responded, telling him everything he needed to know.

When he lifted his head, it was to cloudy gray eyes, tawny skin flushed with warmth, and a full mouth too breathless to close.

"You can afford me, Stevie," he said, his voice rough with emotion. "I'm here anytime you want me—free of charge."

Five

"Free of charge. *Free* of charge. Tell it to the Granby National Bank, Mr. Morgan," Stevie muttered, tightening her one-handed grip on the steering wheel. The Mustang flew down the highway, a red streak burning up the road. Wind whipped through the open window and tangled her hair.

Depositing the week's receipts had barely covered the Trail's outstanding checks, a fact her banker had insisted on dwelling upon—over and over again. The man was uncanny. Inside of five minutes, without her even asking, he'd made it darn clear that her line of credit was drier than a desert in June. He obviously hadn't studied Hal Morgan's theory of economics.

"Free of charge." An unladylike snort summed up her opinion of his offer. Unfortunately, nothing she'd tried in the last three days had been able to negate the effect of his last kiss. With very little effort, she could recall every mesmerizing, emotionally drowning second. She also remembered how she'd kissed him back. The thought alone was enough to bring a blush to her cheeks.

She'd tried to forget how it felt to be held by a man, and it hadn't been too tough. Kip's charm had been his love of fun not his lovemaking, at least not with her—that probably was why he'd left. But Hal Morgan's kisses, the growing spiral of sensuality he so easily pulled her into, refused to be forgotten. Damn him anyway.

The last thing she needed was another man, especially one of the traveling kind. If he thought he could breeze into town and fool around with a country girl for a couple of months, he had another thought coming.

The Mustang roared up behind a slow-moving trailer, and Stevie downshifted, gunning the motor for a burst of speed. The car delivered in seconds and she shot by the vehicle. The action matched her mood, reckless. If she'd had a dime to her name, she'd have turned around and headed the other way, out of the county, out of the state, out of the whole mess. The only thing awaiting her in Grand Lake was a line of suppliers she couldn't pay, and Halsey Morgan. She didn't know how she was going to face either.

Sighing, she put the car back into fourth gear and felt the responsive surge of pure power. A wide, silver ribbon of water flickered between the pine trees bordering the road, the first of the three-lake chain leading into Grand Lake. Midafternoon sunshine streamed over the mountains and turned the high country meadows into fields of greenish-gold, but Stevie didn't see the beauty, only the sameness of a view she'd memorized long ago, a view she'd probably take to the grave unless a financial miracle fell out of the bright blue sky.

Typically, trouble not miracles was lined up in front of the Trail's End. Stevie pulled in next to Hal's hunk-of-junk truck and counted no less than three delivery trucks parked on either side, one for liquor, two for beer. The drivers, she knew, would be chomping at the bit, hanging around like a trio of vultures to pick her checkbook clean.

Another heavy sigh blew from her lips, convincing her to sit in the car for a few minutes until she could find a cheerful mood. She'd take them on one at a time and do her best to talk them out of full payment. No, she thought, she'd do better than her best. If any one of the drivers walked out with more than a hundred of her dollars, she'd buy the bar a round—and she sure as hell couldn't afford that. And Hal Morgan? She'd save him for last, after she had a few successes under her belt.

Straightening her shoulders with a deep breath, she got out of the car and walked into the Trail.

"Hi, Tom, Paul, Garrett. How are you guys doing today?" She deliberately left Hal out of her greeting as she strode into the bar, not trusting herself to look at him without staring at his mouth. Whoever had taught him how to use it hadn't left anything out of the lessons, and despite his sultry-voiced confession, the man hadn't forgotten a move.

Surprisingly, the drivers barely acknowledged her entrance. Tom lifted a hand, almost as if he was shooing her away. Paul mumbled a "Hello." Garrett didn't even give her a glance. The three of them sat at the bar, leaning forward with rapt looks on their faces. Confusion forced her gaze to Hal.

"Afternoon, Stevie Lee. How'd it go?" He was leaning against the cash register, bigger than life and smiling at her with the mouth that haunted her dreams. The rolled-up sleeves of his chambray shirt exposed dark brown forearms and the rhythm of slowly tightening and releasing muscles as he polished yet one more beer mug. Her glassware had never had it so good, she thought with a repressed sigh.

"Fine," she answered noncommittally, watching the drivers out of the corner of her eye, waiting for one of them to pounce. "I'll be in my office if—"

"So, you're hanging there, and you hear that rumbling business," Tom interrupted, his voice practically breathless, his eyes glued on Hal.

Old Tom Hanson breathless? Stevie arched a brow at Hal, and he grinned. Then he did something strange. Under the bar, where the other men couldn't see, he jerked his thumb toward the back room. Confusion complete, her glance darted in the direction of his gesture. Was it a warning? Or was he trying to get rid of her too?

"And the other guy, John what's-his-name, he's slipping away on you," Tom continued, obviously trying to regain Hal's attention. "The rope's a frayin', the wind's a blowin', and ole John's a slippin'."

"And then you hear the rumble," Paul repeated, hunching farther over the bar.

"Yeah, the rumble," Garrett added his two bits, pulling his rag of a cowboy hat further down on his brow.

Hal turned his back to her, blocking her from the men's view, and gave the silent signal again, all the while picking up the threads of his story.

Well, I'll tell you, twenty thousand feet up a Himalayan beauty there's only two places for a rumble to come from, the sky or the mountain, and they're both bad news."

Finally Stevie understood. Without another word, she slipped around the end of the bar and into the hallway. If he wanted to run interference for her, fine, but she doubted if it would work for long.

Ten minutes later, most of it spent on the edge of her office chair, waiting, she silently conceded a point in his favor. Anybody who could hold the vultures at bay was well worth the five bucks an hour she paid. Fifteen minutes later curiosity got the best of her. Quietly she slipped back into the hall, staying out of view but not out of earshot.

". . . the biggest, suckingest hole this side of the Waghi, driving us against the boulder and holding us tight. Charlie yelled 'High side!' and we were scrambling like mad."

Stevie settled against the wall, head cocked to hear every hair-raising twist. In a week of working with him side by side, she'd never heard the same story twice, and although he obviously always survived, he never failed to put enough doubts in her mind to make her wonder each time whether Halsey Morgan would come out alive.

"Ted fell in the river and shot the rapids the hard way, getting tumbled around and bouncing off every rock. Lars went next," Hal's voice softened to a hush, "and that left me and Charlie. I could hear him praying in the back of the raft, and I'll tell you, there's nothing like hearing your team leader praying to shoot your confidence all to hell."

The drivers chuckled in unison, and a wry smile

tilted Stevie's mouth. Tom, she knew, wouldn'
even dip his big toe in Grand Lake, let alone ge
on a river raft.

"So there we were, hanging on that boulder
most of our gear and our buddies floating off int
a jungle, the waves drowning our raft, and Char
lie praying."

The phone jangled in her ear, startling her
Stevie jumped, cussed, and failed to make a rur
for the office.

"Back in a second." Hal cut his story short and
stepped into the hall.

If she only could have disappeared once in he
life, Stevie would have chosen this moment. Bu
she didn't have time to pull the look of surprise
off her face or get out of his way.

"Oops, sorry," he whispered, accidentally knock
ing against her in the small space. He picked up
the phone. "Hello." Then he settled against the
old Frigidaire, trapping her once more.

"Yes. Yes. Well it's nice to talk to you too."

Stevie wondered who he was talking to; she
wondered how to slip by him. She started to move
but he had another idea. Very casually, he stretched
his arm out and rested his hand on the wall be
hind her, bringing them chest to chest, with only
the phone cord between the pearly gray snaps o
his shirt and the blue plaid flannel of hers. The
heat of his body touched her knee, her thigh, the
top of her shoulder. She felt his slow, teasing
smile blush her cheeks.

"A spectacular view," he drawled into the phone
but his gaze remained fixed on her, the indigo
depths of his eyes darkening with appreciatior
and setting off all of her warning bells. She took a
step back, right into the wall.

"Very cozy. Thanks to Stevie Lee . . . yes, she is . . . very nice." The deep roughness of his voice strummed across her emotions and echoed through her breasts as he followed her with a step of his own. Stevie squirmed, but only once, immediately realizing her mistake. His smile broadened, deepening the creases in his dark cheeks and feathering the whiter lines of crow's feet at the corners of his eyes.

"Definitely . . . a wonderful job . . . all kinds of fringe benefits." The lazy, heated track of his gaze over her face came to rest on her mouth, and his own mouth softened, his smile fading. Stevie's heart did a slow slide up into her throat, making it impossible to catch her suddenly disappearing breath.

"Thanks. I'll look forward to meeting you . . . okay, good-bye." Without taking his eyes off of her, he hung up the phone. "Hi, Stevie." He whispered the words across her lips as he bent his head down. "It wasn't the same around here without you today. I missed you."

"Hal, please—"

He never gave her a chance to save herself. His mouth opened over her lips, his hand came up the side of her neck and cupped her face, and his hips rolled into hers, pressing her against the wall and into his heat.

What little rational thought she'd been able to hold onto fled on wings of stolen pleasure. Desire weakened her knees and pulled a gasp from her lungs.

"Yes, Stevie," he urged her on, with his words and the warmth and pressure of his body. Then his tongue delved deep, tasting and giving a sweetness like none she'd ever known.

Stevie sank willingly into the sensual fascination of his kiss, feeling the muscled hardness of him beneath her hands, the gentle, insistent passion in his mouth on hers.

"He looks kind of busy to me." Someone chuckled.

"Real busy."

"Looks like a heap of trouble, if you ask me."

Somewhere, way in the back of her mind, the intrusion registered, but just barely. The ending of the kiss registered completely, though, leaving her with a mess of unfulfilled physical promises, and her hands tangled through the golden silk of his hair.

Tom chuckled again. "Don't mind us."

"Oh, no, not us." Paul repeated.

"We'll catch you next week. You kids carry on." Even the dour Garrett couldn't resist teasing her.

Embarrassed down to the toes of her boots, Stevie opened her eyes and stared over Hal's shoulder at the three older men. They were staring right back, all grinning like a pack of fools.

Tom cackled. "Yep, you kids do carry on. You sure do carry on."

Her eyes flashed to Hal's. He was grinning at her with the best of them.

"Don't forget where we were, Hal. Right there hanging on that rock."

"Old Ted and Lars floating away."

"Charlie praying." The three men each reminded him of a bit of the story.

"I won't forget." He glanced back, lowering his guard for an instant.

It was all Stevie needed. In a second, she dipped under his arm, breaking free. Then she gave the drivers one all-encompassing lethal glare and stomped into the back room.

"Told you it looked like trouble."

"She's been needing that kind of trouble."

"The girl's been alone too long."

If she'd had an office door, "the girl" would have slammed it.

Holding the end of her braid in her mouth, Stevie twisted her back toward the mirror and tried to see what was catching the zipper on her dress. Sunday supper at the ranch with her folks demanded a level of attire she usually avoided, for this very reason.

"Come on, you son of a gun. *Give.*" It did—by coming apart. Stevie stared silently at the broken zipper. Then she sighed and sat down on the edge of the tub, dropping her head into her hands.

What was going on with her life? she wondered, but not for long. The answer came to her in a visual memory of a pair of dark sun-shot eyes, and a body that didn't know when to quit. Halsey Morgan was going on with her life. Since he'd walked into her bar, nothing had gone right, and everything had gone right.

His easygoing charm brought record numbers of customers into the bar. The Trail was breaking new financial ground every week. But he also teased, cajoled, and kissed her. He rocked her tidy plans and sent them tumbling. He touched her and made her feel alive.

"No," she said with a moan, burying her head farther into her arms. She shouldn't want him, need him, think about him all the time. She wouldn't fall in love. Above all, she had to save herself from the ultimate folly. Before she knew it, summer would turn into fall, and Hal would disappear into the great unknown. His kind never stayed in one place too long. And at the rate she was going, she'd be lucky to get to Denver again, let alone anyplace else.

"No, no, no," she whispered into her lap, refusing to accept defeat on any quarter. Somehow the Trail would pull her through, somehow she'd hold on to her senses.

A cold wet nose nudging her arm reminded her of the time. "Okay, Tiva. You're right, we're already late." She lifted her head and reached out to scratch the husky's muzzle, rubbing her fingers up the white mask of fur to a special spot behind the dog's ears. Tiva groaned in pleasure and shoved her head into Stevie's lap. "Now look at you. I thought you wanted to get going," she said. "Your buddy Blue is waiting, hmmm, with her new puppies. And so is Mom's fried chicken."

The pitiful state of Stevie's wardrobe limited her choices to her wedding dress—an unlikely choice for supper—and a mid-calf length skirt. Black, with a deep yoke and lots of tiny buttons up the front, it flowed around her legs. She slipped it over her cream-colored cowboy boots, and pulled on the matching western style shirt. A fancy leather belt with her name scrolled across the back finished the outfit.

She grabbed Kip's leather bomber jacket on her way out the door. In a typically dramatic gesture, he'd left it the night he walked out on her, promising someday to return and retrieve them both— after he'd worked a few things out, such as the blonde waiting in his car, she'd guessed at the time—after he'd grown up a bit and was ready to settle down, he'd said. After hell freezes over, Stevie had replied.

The last she'd heard, the blonde was now a red-head, Kip still hadn't grown up, and as far as she knew hell hadn't frozen over.

Tiva raced down the road leading to the ranch, and Stevie let her run. The evening sun slanted shadows beneath the pines, and dappled the soft green leaves on a stand of aspens. Stevie's boots crunched along the dirt and gravel road, her long legs carrying her quickly through the quarter mile of forest to the top of a rise.

A broad, thickly-grassed pasture stretched out on the other side, filled with grazing cattle and a few mule deer passing through. The Bar Rocking C ranch house was another quarter mile up the meadow on the north end, and dotted here and there across the two hundred acres were the homes of her brothers.

A variety of trucks and cars were in the drive-way, and Stevie speeded up her gait, realizing she was the last to arrive. Later in the summer when the weather warmed up, the clan would gather on the front porch until supper, but the coolness of early June kept everyone inside tonight.

Warmth and laughter surrounded her as she opened the heavy oak door. It spilled out of the house from the expansive, pine-paneled living room. A rock fireplace took up one wall, and worn, but much-loved furniture was scattered here and there.

Stevie hung her coat on a rack by the door, between Nola's rabbit fur jacket and a white, quilted parka, and turned toward the kitchen. Then the color and style of the parka registered in her mind. Stevie jerked her head around. It couldn't be, but it had to be.

Her mind flashed back to the phone call he'd

gotten, and she knew that somehow, some way, for whatever reason, her mother had invited Halsey Morgan to Sunday supper. Without a second thought, she grabbed her coat off the hook. She'd call from her cabin and tell them she was sick, tell them Tiva was sick. No, she instantly changed her mind, that would only bring her mother running. She'd call Francine and have her beg Doug to take her out, and then she'd have to go fill in at the Trail. Or maybe she'd . . .

"Hey, everybody. Stevie's here." John, her oldest brother, peeked around the archway from the kitchen. "Hurry up, Stevie. We're all starving. You know how the kids get."

Caught with her arms half in her coat, Stevie pretended they were half out, knowing no excuse would get by her mother if she had to lie to her face. Resigned, she rehung her coat and walked on leaden feet into the big country kitchen. The whole family sat around the dining room table—the whole family and one golden-haired, blue-eyed guest.

"Hi, Stevie."

"Stevie Lee."

"Stevie." A hodgepodge of siblings and their spouses acknowledged her arrival with a lift of the hand here, a smile there.

"Hi, Stutz. How's my girl?" Her father smiled up at her from the head of the table. His dark brown hair showed signs of age in the sprinkling of gray at his temples.

Stevie hazarded a glance in Hal's direction, and saw his eyebrows rise at her dad's greeting, then rise even farther when her mother spoke.

"Stephanie Lisa Marie, where have you been? We thought we were going to have to send one of the boys up for you. Your Mr. Morgan must be thinking we never eat around here. Now don't you come in empty-handed. Go ahead and get the biscuits out of the oven. Nola and Sally, help me with the chicken and stuff. John, why don't you get everybody another beer." Elizabeth Carson bustled around the table, a cloud of flour following her every step. "Diana, you stay put, dear. We don't want that baby coming before its time. Gene, go tell the children that their Aunt Stephanie finally made it."

Her Mr. Morgan watched the Carsons hurry this way and that, an amused smile crooking the corner of his mouth. Stevie wanted to groan—quite loudly—throw her hands up in the air, and leave. Instead she obeyed every maternal command, piling a couple of dozen buttermilk biscuits into a linen-lined basket and running to the pantry for three kinds of jam.

By the time she returned, only one empty chair remained, the one next to Hal. She should have seen the bit of maneuvering coming down the pike; her mother was nothing if not predictable. Plastering a false smile to her face, she sat down and ignored him the best she could—an impossible endeavor.

"Hi, Stephanie Lisa Marie," his deep voice whispered below the noise. "I would have waited and walked you down, but I didn't want to scare you off."

Keeping her gaze firmly on the napkin she was unfolding in her lap, Stevie began an appropriately stiff reply—rudeness being her last defense—but got no further than the necessary intake of breath before she noticed the nine pairs of eyes trained on them. Damn him anyway. If he'd yelled at her, no one would have noticed. But no, Hal Morgan had to whisper, had to enclose the two of them in a cocoon of intimacy with his rough voice and the incline of his head.

"Don't give it another thought, Hal. We probably would have ended up talking business, and you know how boring that can be." The words fell from the tight line of her mouth, fooling no one.

"Mother? Will you lead the prayer?" Richard Carson requested.

Nine pairs of eyes closed. The tenth and eleventh pairs locked onto each other—the gray ones wide with alarm, the blue ones twinkling with mischief.

"Dear heavenly Father, thank you for the bounty and the blessings of our lives . . ." Elizabeth intoned in her sweet, melodic voice.

Dear Lord, don't let him shout out, Stevie privately prayed alongside her mother. As the "Amens" came closer and closer, she wrapped her hands around each other tighter and tighter, steeling herself for the worst.

". . . please watch over our dear Diana as she brings another of your sweet blessings into our lives. We'd like a girl this time, Lord." Mother Carson and the Lord were on very personal terms, allowing for a number of special requests over the years. Not so surprisingly, the good Lord had granted most of them, a fact Elizabeth never let pass without her gratitude. ". . . and thank you, especially, for bringing Mr. Morgan back into the safety of your fold. Our prayers have been with him these many years while he was lost in pagan, tropical lands . . ."

The heavenly message resounded in Stevie's heart and mind, turning her emotions inside out and filling her with pure, unadulterated guilt. Her chin dropped lower to her chest. Her shoulders slumped in heartfelt penance. She'd virtually banked on his death or disappearance, and then he'd come out of nowhere and filled her life with his own, making every day new again.

Suddenly she knew she didn't want him to leave. The sheer force of the realization frightened her. How had such a thing happened? When had she become so vulnerable?

As if sensing her distress, a large, calloused hand reached over and covered hers. His thumb brushed across her skin. She wanted to pull away, meant to pull away, but the forgiveness and understanding in his touch held her captive in his grasp.

Daring all, she opened her eyes and found him quietly in prayer, his thick dark lashes resting on his cheeks, his mouth moving in unspoken words. Gently he twined his fingers through hers and pulled her hand into his lap.

Lord help her, she thought, her eyes drifting closed. She was falling in love.

Six

Love? There had to be a mistake, or so Stevie kept telling herself all through dinner, all through dessert, and all through the following hour of chit-chat in the living room.

"No," she whispered, staring into her lap. She had to have more brains than to fall in love. A little physical attraction? Fine, she'd concede to attraction. But love?

"No," she decided aloud with another whisper. Just because he was crazy and fun, gorgeous and passionate, and had lived, actually lived, the life of her dreams was no reason to go falling in—

"Stephanie? Stephanie, dear." The sound of her mother's voice broke into the middle of her silent argument.

"What?" She lifted her head and found all the Carson women looking at her. After dinner the men had gone outside to kick tires and lean on fence posts. The ladies had retired to the living room, and from the sofa to the piano bench to the overstuffed chairs flanking the fireplace, they were all looking at her.

Elizabeth clasped her hands in her flour-dusted lap and leaned forward, her head inclined to an inquisitive angle. "Dear, you've been mumbling to yourself over there for nearly a half an hour, and frankly, it's starting to worry me. Are you feeling all right "

"Fine, Mom. I'm feeling fine. It's summer, that's all. You know, long hours, lots of business." Stevie hedged around the truth, far from ready to accept it herself.

"I think it's something else," Nola said in a singsongy voice, plunking out a few notes on the piano.

From one of the doily-covered chairs, Diana chuckled in agreement. The soft laughter flushed her cheeks and shook her gently rounded tummy. "My, my, I never thought I'd see the day. I think our Stevie is—"

"Fine, Mom. Just fine," Stevie quickly interjected, throwing both of the other women silencing glares.

"Are you sick, Aunt Stevie?" A little voice asked.

"No, Josh. I'm fine,' she reassured her three-year-old nephew, beginning to feel like a broken record.

"Oh," Josh's pink mouth rounded. Then he went back to running his matchbox truck over the blue cotton of his grandmother's dress, using the pleats as drag strips and her apron as a grandstand. G.I. Joe and He-Man shared one floury pocket. A passel of Thundercats shared another.

She saw her mother gearing up for another question, but she was interrupted by the returning men.

"Elizabeth, where did I put them new truck

keys. Hal here is going to take it for a spin. The boy's never driven a king cab with dual rear wheels before. I told him there's nothing like it, nothing like it"—her father rummaged around the cluttered top of the ranch's accounting desk—"but I'll be danged if I can remember what I did with the keys."

"They're in your pocket, dear."

Without the slightest embarrassment, Richard Carson dug into his pocket and came up with the keys. "Now be gentle with her, Hal. Ease her out of first, try the wheel a little until you get the hang of her. Test 'em out first, that's what I always say. Keeps you from running into a brick wall."

Mischievous indigo eyes flashed at Stevie from across the living room. "You're a man after my own heart, Rich. I always test the waters before I jump in."

"Hah!" Stevie whispered under her breath, not believing a word of it. Neither could she believe her father was giving him the keys to his new truck. Hal must have scored a grand slam on her father's character scale.

"Tsk, tsk, Stevie Lee." Nola crooned softly, running her fingers over the piano keys to keep anyone else from hearing. "Didn't he test your waters first?"

Stevie opened her mouth to protest, but her never-subtle sister forged ahead. "Doug told me all about your little tête-à-tête in the office at the Trail. Sounds like fun." A bar of the wedding march slipped in under a lightly played hymn.

Panic urged Stevie to her feet. "I have to leave," she blurted out.

"Yes, dear, you should be home in bed." Elizabeth stood up, absently arranging the muscle-bound, plastic figures in her apron pockets to keep them from falling out. "Let me get you a quart of soup out of the freezer."

"Are you sick, Stutz?"

"No, Dad, I'm . . . fine."

"I don't know, honey. You are looking a mite peaked. Hal, why don't you give my girl a ride home? I'll walk up and get the truck in the morning. Elizabeth," Richard called, following her mother out of the room. "Why don't you get a quart for Hal too. The boy's been living on raw fish. . . ." His voice trailed off as he entered the kitchen.

The evening's good-byes proved to be a drawn out affair. John and Diana bundled Josh into their truck for the short haul home up the meadow. Nola and her husband, Bob, rounded up their eight-year-old son, Ryan, and brushed a ton of hay out of his hair before settling him into their car for the ride into town. They didn't get ten yards before Nola jumped out of the cab and returned one of Blue's puppies to the barn. Gene, the bachelor sheriff, walked home.

Long after they'd all left, Hal and Stevie were still loading food into the back of the truck.

"I never cut 'em less than an inch thick. Not even in the lean times, did I, Mother?" Richard handed Hal a bundle of T-bone steaks wrapped in butcher paper.

"Never, dear. Hal? Did you say you liked cherry pie or apple pie best?"

"Apple, ma'am, but—"

"Save your breath," Stevie said with a sigh, standing by his side. "They won't be happy until you're pushing the scale at two hundred pounds."

At his look of alarm, she found a smile. "Hey,

don't blame me. you brought this on yourself, talking about raw fish and coconut milk."

"Yeah, but I was good at getting both of them. I didn't think I looked underfed."

"It has nothing to do with how you look. You look great. . . ." *Oh, brother.* Stevie dropped her head into her hand, mortified to the pointy toes of her boots.

"Thanks." He leaned in close and whispered in her ear. "I think you look great, too, and I can't wait to get you alone so I can—"

"Now you bake this at four hundred degrees for about fifteen minutes or so, then finish it off at three fifty." Elizabeth came around the side of the truck, carrying a homemade frozen pie. Stevie took the opportunity to slip away from him, for all the good it did her. The inside of a truck's cab, even a king cab, didn't allow for much of an escape. There seemed to be no getting away from Halsey Morgan.

Elizabeth continued her instructions. "I'm going to set this on the seat so it doesn't get banged around. Then you kids better get going. A little cheese is always good on apple pie, Hal, ups the nutrition. Don't put it on all at once, though. Melt a bit on a piece just before you eat it."

"Thank you, ma'am. I will." Above her mother's head, Hal caught Stevie's eye and slowly smiled, one of his heart-stopping, midnight smiles, the kind that always reminded her of his kisses. A flash of warmth raced across her cheeks and down her body, and Stevie prayed, *Dear God, let me get home without making a fool of myself.*

His whispered promise and the smile were enough to keep her well to her own side of the seat as they rumbled along the rutted road leading from the ranch to their cabins. Tiva paced the bed of the truck, her muzzle pointed into the night air, her nails pitter-pattering over the metal. Inside the cab, her mistress performed her own version of nervous pattering. She smoothed her damp palms over her skirt, flattening all the wrinkles out of the black cotton. She tucked a few straying tendrils of hair behind her ear. She reached to straighten the collar on her jacket.

"You're fidgeting."

Her fingers froze on the lamb's wool lapel. "No, I'm not. I'm—"

"Fidgeting."

Slowly she uncurled her hands and forced them to relax in her lap. "I'm warm, that's all. I was just . . . warm."

"Right," he said in a slow drawl, shooting her a wry glance. "We're having a regular heat wave."

Even as he spoke, a light skiff of snow began falling from the sky, winding its way through the trees, drifting past the headlights, and blowing across the road. She couldn't win.

"Yessiree, a regular heat wave." The fact that the weather was making a fool of her brought a smile to his mouth. "Stutz, huh? Where did he get that?"

"Bear cat."

"I should have guessed." he chuckled softly, obviously agreeing with her father's summation.

Squeezed up close to the door, Stevie hazarded a quick glance at him from beneath her lashes—and found her gaze lingering long after the word "quick" lost all meaning. Moonlight streamed through the windshield, turning his hair into a mane of silver-gold and casting the broad features of his face into soft shadow. Unaware of her surreptitious fascination, he leaned back in the seat and tightened his large, calloused hands on the steering wheel. The action reminded her of the night they'd met, the ease with which he'd used one punch to free her from Kong. The big man hadn't been back to his favorite watering hole since. Stevie figured he probably was more embarrassed than afraid, but she'd also heard he'd stayed in bed for two days trying to recover. Certainly no one else in town had even made a peep at her since Halsey Morgan had shown up.

How long would she miss him when he was gone? she wondered, already feeling the beginnings of loneliness. How long would she remember the wild mélange of colors streaked through his hair, the way his eyes turned from a dark slate-blue to almost aqua in the sunlight, and the way they darkened again when he smiled his midnight smiles?

Forever. The answer came quickly and easily with the sudden memory of his kisses. Each and every one played across her mind, teasing her body with forbidden fantasies. Stevie tried to dampen them, but they insisted on feeling real— the touch of his mouth softening hers, the caress of his lips as he whispered sensual promises in her ear, the hardness of his body beneath her hands.

She clenched her fingers and forced her gaze away from him. Regardless of the effort, her imagination continued heating up to the point where she really was warm—warm, dismayed, and ready to run. After Kip had left, she'd rather forgotten about sex. There had never been time to worry over her lack of a physical involvement, nor had anyone in Grand Lake brought it to mind—until

Halsey Morgan. His presence shattered her sterile existence and filled her with all kinds of longings, not only for his stories of adventure and travel, and his laughter and the niceness of just having him around, but for his body—every muscled inch of it.

Okay, Stevie. Get a hold of yourself. Calm down, she silently commanded. There was a world of difference between the relatively chaste mess she'd landed her heart in, and the potentially devastating pain of giving herself completely away to him. For he wanted her completely, of that she had no doubts. Every time he touched her, his message and intent were crystal clear.

The truck rounded the last bend into her driveway, revealing a three-quarter moon hanging in the cloudy night sky. Stars were scattered across the heavens, mixing their light with the falling snow. Hal slowed the truck, coming to a gradual stop, but before he could turn off the engine, Stevie opened the door.

"Thanks. Thanks for the ride." The words came quick and breathless on the tail end of her decision to make a run for it. The instant she found a firm footing, she bolted.

Hal didn't waste a second on his confusion. He slammed on the parking brake, jumped out of the truck, and caught her on the back porch.

"Hey, wait a minute . . . wait a minute. Please." His chest heaved beneath his sweater. His breath vaporized into cloudy puffs in the air.

"Hal, I have to go." Stevie fumbled with her keys.

"No, you don't."

"I have to work in the morning." The ring of keys jangled and jumbled in her hands, none of them looking even vaguely familiar.

"No, you don't."

"I have to—"

"Stevie." His patient tone put a halt to her fumbling. "All you have to do, all you're going to do, is tell me what's wrong. You hardly touched your dinner, and what you did to your mother's pecan pie was sacrilege, mashing it around like mud."

Wide gray eyes lifted to his, sparkling in the moonlight, and telegraphing a confusion that put his to shame.

"What's wrong?" he demanded softly, his hands gripping both of her arms.

"I'm in love," she choked the words out, making the condition sound like the voice of doom. Lying to him never crossed her mind. She'd been moseying around and backing away from the truth all night, and it hadn't done her a darn bit of good; she'd still run smack-dab into love.

Her confession stopped Hal's heart cold, a feeling he'd had many times when hanging from the end of a rope or facing a bevy of suspicious border guards, but never when standing on firm ground with only one, harmless woman. The realization hit him with the impact of a gale force wind. Sweet Stevie Lee Brown had gotten to him, really gotten to him, and while he'd been fooling around, she'd gone and fallen in love with somebody else.

"Who is he?" The harshness of his voice echoed the sudden, awful emptiness he felt.

Without replying, she bowed her head. A cascade of honey-brown hair fell out of her french braid, obscuring her face from his searching gaze.

"Dammit, Stevie. Tell me." His hands tightened around her arms, pulling her up and closer. "Tell me."

"You." The merest breath of a whisper carried

the word through the night air, so quietly Hal was sure he'd heard wrong.

"Who?"

"You."

"Me?"

Nodding in confirmation, she turned her head sideways, avoiding his eyes.

Hal held her, staring down at the snow-dusted cap of silky hair streaming around her face, and slowly his anger melted into wonder. "Are you sure?"

"Pretty sure," she murmured, a forlorn sigh trembling her shoulders.

He felt the tremor beneath his fingers; he heard the sadness in her voice, and they left him at a complete and total emotional loss. The wind blew around them, gusting up the snow and creaking through the trees, the only sound breaking the silence until he found the courage to speak, ever so softly.

"Is it that terrible? Being in love with me?"

"Yes." The quietest whisper she'd made yet gave him the answer he didn't want to hear.

"Ah, Stevie," he said, moaning, pulling her into the warmth of his arms. He buried his head in the curve of her neck. Under her jacket, his hands spread across her back and drew her even closer. She loved him, and it was breaking her heart— nothing in his lifetime of experiences had prepared him for the bitter sweetness of such a love. So he held her, gently, feeling benighted and bewildered.

Stevie sunk against his chest, resting her cheek on his sweater, allowing herself one moment of weakness. She felt so awful.

Hal struggled with the temptation of having her

close, her heart beating next to his, her scent
filling his mind and body with desire, her softness pressed against his hardness. She loved him
he wanted her, a seemingly simple combination—
but nothing he came up with in his mind could
bridge the gap between the two. Her love was a
gift unlike any he'd ever received, much too precious to misuse.

He'd been ready to take her into his bed since
the first night they'd met. He was ready now. His
body ached with the want and need to have her
beside him, to run his hands across the silkiness
of her bare skin, to follow those sentient move-
ments with his mouth until she touched him in
return.

"I have to go," he said abruptly, quietly, interrupting the erotic drift of his thoughts. The softness of her neck beckoned to his lips and tongue.
She was so close, only a slight movement would
bring him into contact and destroy all his good
intentions. "I have to go," he repeated louder,
hoping to break the lethargy invading his limbs.

"Yes." She took a step backward, and Hal released her, reluctance making his hands linger on
her waist.

This time she had no trouble finding the right
key. He watched her leave him and waited until
he heard the click of the lock falling in place, all
the while fighting the urge to pull her back into
his arms. She loved him; it would be so easy—
and so wrong.

From the darkness of her living room, Stevi
watched him walk down the meadow, a strange
tightness in her chest increasing with each step
he took. Light from the moon fell upon his swept-
back, shaggy golden hair and glittered across the

diamond pattern of his parka. Tiva followed him down to his cabin, the white underside of her tail lashing like a flag in the night. Even her dog had deserted her. Letting out a pained sigh, Stevie forced herself away from the window.

If he was doing the right thing, why did he feel like the world's biggest fool? Hal shoved the last of the steaks into his freezer and hung on the refrigerator door, pondering the question. The answer he came up with made no sense. If he loved her, wouldn't he be the first to know?

Maybe not, he silently admitted. Love wasn't exactly his area of expertise. He'd never stayed in one place long enough to fall in love with anybody. Another moment of thought showed him the faulty logic behind his line of reasoning. After his months on the island, he'd seen lots of women in Hawaii, California, Nevada, Utah, but he hadn't gotten turned on until he'd walked into the back room of a shabby bar in Grand Lake, Colorado. What had it been? A minute, maybe two? And he'd been ready to make love to a complete stranger. A stranger with wild eyes and a ton of dynamite packed into a red shirt and a pair of jeans.

"Sweet Allah," he muttered under his breath. If love felt wonderful and awful at the same time, if love was sleepless nights and waking fantasies, then this was it. No wonder he'd felt turned inside out and upside down every time he looked at her. No wonder he could do little else but look at her constantly. And when she wasn't with him, all he did was think about her.

"Por Dios." He needed to think, to find an angle on this new and amazing situation. Grabbing a couple of beers, he headed for the front porch. He always thought better with nothing but the sky

above him. His good friend Mother Nature had
given him most of his answers to life's deeper
questions. He hoped she wouldn't let him down
tonight.

Stevie tossed and turned in her bed in a vain
attempt to find comfort. She refluffed her pillows
with a vengeance, but all they did was fluff right
back at her, refusing to become the sanctuary she
needed for her aching head. Finally, beaten by her
own inner turmoil, she flopped back on the sheets
and stared at the ceiling.

Subdued light from the cloud-covered moon
tracked the curved pine boards and became lost
in the high arch, but no more lost than she was
in her loneliness. Halsey Morgan *was* alive. The
sight and scent and feel of him resonated in her
every pulse. They suffused her veins and filled her
mind with his presence. Yet her arms remained
empty.

Weakly, she pulled a pillow across her chest and
hugged it tight. What would she do now? Tiptoe
around him until he left? For leave he would
she'd never doubted or underestimated his yen
for wandering. The faraway places of the world
pulled him like a magnet. They pulled her, too,
but for whatever reasons, she had feet of clay
compared to his nomadic ways. He got up and left
when the next port called; she got up and went to
work every day. Day after day after day.

She sighed and rolled over onto her stomach,
propping her chin up with a pillow. The head
board of her bed proved as boring as the ceiling.
She would fire him, she thought, then immedi
ately discarded the idea. He was much to valuable
to her bottom line for her to throw him away.
Hiring him had been her only smart move since

he'd met him. And could she really keep her sanity, knowing he was in town and not where he could see him every day?

"No," she whispered forlornly, rolling to her back and taking the pillow with her.

Somewhere off in the night a coyote yapped its freedom at the moon. The clear, wild call broke the stillness of the sky, echoing through her room and catching at her dreams. She tilted her head up off the pillow and held herself quiet, waiting for the answering call. When it came, it was much closer and much more familiar. Before the cry died out, she was on her feet. Tiva had enough wildness in her to run after her feral brothers, but she didn't have the sense to find her way home. Stevie had lost enough of her life in the last few weeks; she wasn't about to lose her dog too.

Clutching her flannel nightgown up off the floor, Stevie took the stairs two at a time and raced across the living room. Halfway to the door, a third voice joined the others and stopped her dead in her tracks. The last song rose in a long howl, deeper and rougher and infinitely more emotional than those that had gone before. The sound curled around her heart and sent a tremor down her spine. She stood in the darkness, listening as the three animals called to each other in a repeating chorus of "Oy, oy, oyuuuuu." One coyote, one dog— and one man.

On quiet feet, Stevie moved toward the window. She touched the cold pane of glass with her fingertips, listening to the sonorous refrains fill the air, her eyes finding him without err. Sitting on the edge of his porch, knees splayed, his head thrown back, Hal howled up at the stars. One of

his arms rested across the husky's back. He hel
a bottle of beer in his other hand, wetting hi
throat after each encore. Tiva went next, pickin
up the song as Hal finished, adding her sopran
to his tenor. Then they both waited, heads cocke
and soon the coyote's voice cut through the nigh
echoing off the mountains and hills.

The wildest call brought a wide grin to his fac
He reached up to scratch the husky behind th
ear, and then lowered his nose to hers. By Tiva
reaction, Stevie knew he was talking to her, cor
ferring with her in his gravelly voice, and she fe
the oddest pang of jealousy. As if coming to
mutual agreement with his canine buddy, Ha
laughed and tilted his head back once more. Moor
light rippled through his hair and shone alon
the column of his throat. Next to his golden, ma;
culine beauty, Tiva's coat glistened with a silver
darkness.

The two of them made quite a team, howling u
at the sky and playing backup to the coyote, qui
a team indeed. They were having fun just bein
together and being a part of the universe. The
naturalness, their easy camaraderie, brought he
own solitude into a sharp and painful focus. Stev
took her hand off the window and brushed at he
cheek. She wouldn't cry for him. She'd work wit
him. She'd laugh with him. She'd watch him lea\
at summer's end—and she'd love him until sf
forgot how. But she wouldn't let him hurt her-
she wouldn't cry for him.

Seven

If this was love, Hal didn't know what all the shouting was about. Hell, he'd had a better time dragging himself and a bitchy camel across the Sahara. Not even Delilah had given him as much trouble as Stevie Lee Brown. All his life he'd grappled with Mother Nature's dangers and extremes, the searing heat of the deserts, the endless emptiness of the ocean, the uninhabitable ramparts of the highest mountains, and none of them compared with the whirlwind of emotions Stevie had sucked him into. He didn't know which end was up anymore.

". . . and make sure you clean out the beer cooler tonight after closing, or before, if you find the time."

An unlikely possibility, he thought wryly, looking down at the black cowboy hat pulled low on her forehead and the wealth of hair spilling over her shoulders. He'd never seen her hair unbound before, and it was prettier and silkier than he'd imagined, strands of gold and brown woven together all the way to her waist, skimming the tight curve of her jeans, begging him to gather it up in his hands.

Don't do it, Hal, he warned himself. Another rejection was the last thing he needed, especially in front of the dozen or so regular barflies who were watching Stevie order him around.

She crossed beer cooler off her legal pad without making a dent in the long list of projects she had lined up for him. "Tomorrow see if you can fix the legs on those other two chairs in the office. We're going to need all the seating we can get for the Buffalo Barbecue. I'll get Doug to work on the broken table."

With effort, Hal kept his hands and a smart remark to himself. He'd seen Doug's handiwork. Anything her brother fixed Hal usually had to fix again. For an engineering major, the kid was remarkably klutzy when it came to putting things back together.

She crossed off chairs and scribbled his initials next to the item. "On Thursday night we'll all put in an extra hour and make sure the liquor is in order. We're not going to have time to hunt around for stuff once the weekend starts. The Fourth of July will make Memorial Day look like a cakewalk."

Three weeks before, Hal would have cringed at the thought of horrendous crowds descending on the Trail again. But not even Stevie could keep up with him now. Or was that the other way around? Since the night she'd told him of her love, she'd put new meaning into the word "avoid" and driven him crazy in the bargain. Too late he'd realized he'd made a big mistake when he'd conned her into giving him a job. By working for her, he'd clipped his own wings. If she wanted to keep her distance, all she had to do was chalk his name up on the schedule and head the other way. She was getting damn good at both. The locals, he knew, were having a heyday watching him come up scoreless time after time in this battle of wills with Stevie Lee. Fortunately for them, they had enough sense to keep their ribald chuckles and comments to themselves. Hal had fielded them for a while, but he wasn't in the mood anymore.

"Okay, I think that's it for now." She ran her pencil down the list, checking one more time. "Any questions?"

Questions? He had a million of them. He started with the one at the top of his own list, hating his curiosity and still not able to keep his mouth shut. "Where are you going?"

"To The Emporium, to have a drink with Jake," she answered, for the fifth night in a row. "The number is posted by the phone."

"I know where the damn number is." Hours of steaming around the Trail working himself into a knot had given him plenty of time to memorize the four numbers necessary to dial a local connection. He was getting damn tired of this game—her running off with the crowds, leaving him alone to clean up and imagine all sorts of goings-on down at The Emporium.

"Good. If you run into trouble, just give a call. I can be back in under five minutes."

"I'm already in trouble," he said under his breath.

At that she glanced up, but typically not at him. "The guy at the end of the bar looks ready for another beer"—turning her head, she checked out the rest of the room—"and everybody else looks fine. I think you can handle it," she said coolly, galling him to the core.

"Dammit, Stevie," he hissed through clenched teeth, quickly coming to the point where he didn't care how many people saw him shot down. "You know what I mean."

Oh, she knew what he meant all right. Dark circles under her eyes attested to the same restless yearnings that were putting the ragged edge to his voice. In the last month she'd dropped ten pounds she could ill afford to lose, causing her mother to cluck alarmingly every time they met.

"No, I don't," she lied, gathering her legal pad to her chest and turning to leave.

She got no farther than the two steps to the hall before she felt his hand on her arm, propelling her forward into the office. Catcalls from the bar followed them.

"Go for it, Hal."

"Hold him off, Stevie."

"If she turns you down again, I'm still here, honey," a smoky, feminine voice crooned, jarring Stevie out of her icy calm. She knew without looking who had spoken, the well-endowed, petite and pretty blonde who hadn't missed a night at the Trail since Hal had started working.

Common sense told her not to care, but it was jealousy that put the acid on her tongue. "Better be careful, *honey*. You wouldn't want to offend your biggest tipper."

Much to her surprise, Hal laughed, still pushing her forward through the hallway. The deep, throaty sound rolled over her like hot honey, reminding her of all the things she was forcing herself to forget. "Now we're getting somewhere, darlin'."

"No, we're not," she said, stumbling to keep a step ahead of him. Showing any emotion was a mistake, and showing jealousy was the biggest mistake of all. "I'm going to The Emporium, and you're staying—"

He swept her into the office, whirling her around in his arms and stealing her breath. "Right here with you, until we work this out," he informed her with a dangerous glint in his eyes, pressing her back against the wall, trapping her with his body, and pushing her pulse into overdrive. "I'll fight with you if you want to fight. I'll make love with you if you want to make love. But I'm through with letting you pretend I'm not here. So what's it going to be, Stevie Lee?" he demanded. "Fighting . . . or loving?"

The pressure of his thigh against hers, the sultry roughness of his voice, left no doubts about his preference, and left her scrambling for a shred of composure. One more kiss, and she'd never survive with her heart intact.

"Fighting," she whispered, looking at the floor, her desk, off into space, anyplace except into those truth-seeking indigo eyes.

"Wrong answer, sweetheart. I'll give you another shot at it." In one smooth move he slipped her hat back off her head, letting it fall to the floor, and ran his hand down the side of her face, brushing her hair away with his fingers.

"Hal—" The warmth of his touch raced across her skin, the gentleness melted away another layer of her protective ice. Lowering her guard, she looked up—her second mistake.

Fathomless blue eyes caressed her face, the lines of strain at the corners softened with each moment his gaze lingered on her mouth. Light from the single lamp on the desk shone through the golden arcs of hair framing his face and sweeping around his collar. Slowly he lifted his gaze and captured a fleeting moment of desire she hadn't been able to control. A heavy sigh swelled his chest.

"Stevie," he drew her name out on a husky breath. "I don't know why you're running so fast and hard . . . but you'll never run fast enough . . . or hard enough to get away from me."

"Leave it alone, Hal," she pleaded softly, even as his warmth and nearness drew her closer to the edge of desire.

"I can't."

"Yes, you can. Just walk away." She shifted her gaze slightly, not wanting him to see her doubts. She had to get out of there before her armor completely fell apart, before she took what he offered, a night of love, maybe a summer. But not the forever she needed. "I have to go. Jake's waiting," she whispered, the lies coming harder.

His other hand slid up her arm and cupped her chin, forcing her to look at him. The dark wings of his eyebrows furrowed above his slate-blue eyes. A pulse of tension beat along the hard angle of his jaw. "If I believed you, even for a moment, I'd let you go." He brushed his thumb across her lower lip, tantalizing the soft flesh, and his voice lowered to a rough timbre. "If I believed you, Stevie . . . if I believed you . . ." the words trailed off as he tilted his head lower and claimed her mouth with his own.

His body came up slowly and solidly against hers, overwhelming her senses with the intensity of his need, the power of his arms wrapping around her, the pure eroticism of his kiss. And once again she sank into the sweet valley where reason had no hold. He slipped his leg between hers and pulled her up his thigh until their hips met, drawing her into a higher level of instantaneous pleasure, a stronger level of need, his mouth never stopping the wet, deep searching of hers.

Stevie gasped at the explosion of sensation he incited with the gentle rocking of her body on his. Shock waves of desire coursed over her in a pulsing rhythm, one after the other, leaving her dazed and hungry for more. Her hands grasped at his shoulders, her mouth opened wider under his, and the rest of her melted into the surrounding strength of his hard body.

Hal cursed himself for a fool, and still he couldn't stop kissing her, holding her, teasing her with his hands and hips. A degree of pressure here, a slight thrust there, every move he made brought a whimper of pleasure from her mouth into his and drove him wild. She was hot and soft in his arms, giving as much as she got—and he was giving her everything. Everything except what they both needed, everything except what he couldn't give her there. He tangled his hands through her hair, and felt her do the same, her fingers tunnelling along the back of his neck and holding him for the sweet invasion of her tongue into his mouth.

He groaned, letting her have her way. It wasn't enough, it could never be enough. He jerked her shirt from her jeans and slid his hand up inside to cup her breast. The heavy fullness, the satin and lace, set him on fire. He reached for the top button of her jeans.

"Hey, Hal. I poured the guys a beer, but Arlene wants a man . . . hattan." Hal's head snapped up. His hand stopped just inside Stevie's waistband. "Sorry, I'll . . . uh . . . get her something." The young man backed off, blushing to the roots of his sandy brown hair.

"Damn," Hal said tightly.

"They're having a management meeting." He heard the boy explain at the bar.

"Right," a masculine voice drawled, his voice easily carrying the short distance into the back room. "I wouldn't mind *meeting* with Stevie Lee myself."

"Forget the manhattan, Pete," Arlene said with a heavy sigh. "I think I'll head up to The Emporium."

Hal turned back to the pale, stricken face of the woman in his arms, on his thigh, wrapped around his neck. Never before at a loss for words, he didn't know where to begin. He should have stopped, he should never have started. "Stevie, I'm sorry."

Her mouth opened, but nothing came out, and slowly her wide, gray eyes filled with tears.

"Hey," he said softly. "It's not that bad." He attempted a smile and failed miserably. His heart was still pounding too fast, his body was still alive with wanting her. He had to let her go, but his hands refused. It took the lone track of a tear over her tawny cheek to convince them. But he no sooner lightened his grip, than she fled, disappearing into the hall before he reacted.

With a stifled groan from way back in his throat, he slammed his fist into the wall—and he let her go on running.

Stevie heard the crash of bottles, the sound spurring her to grab her jacket and run through the bar and into the street. On the boardwalk, she stopped, not sure which way to go. Wind gusted up and matted long tendrils of hair to her damp face. Her breath caught in her throat on the continuous sobs heaving her chest. Forget her heart, she'd lost her mind under his relentless seduction. She'd never felt anything like the physical frenzy he aroused and inflamed inside her. She must be crazy.

She was no virgin. She knew what men and women did together. At least she had thought she knew. Kip had been kind, loving, but he'd never triggered a response even half as passionate as Hal had. The man knew how to caress with his whole body, he knew how to touch her, how to kiss her. Lord, he knew how to kiss her, how to turn a mere meeting of mouths into a sexual experience of the highest order. In comparison she felt naive, even foolish. When all was said and done, Nola was right, her little sister couldn't handle Halsey Morgan.

Stevie lowered her head into her hands and breathed deeply of the cool mountain air. If Pete had shown up even a minute later, he would have caught her with her pants down, literally. Acutely embarrassed by the thought, she dropped her hands and began shoving her shirt back into her jeans. Only half-tidied, she put her legs in motion, making tracks away from the Trail, and headed toward the noise and crowds of The Emporium. She wasn't ready to face herself, not yet.

Hal closed the bar in under five minutes, a new record, and said to hell with fixing chairs, cleaning coolers, and restocking liquor. He needed to find Stevie, he needed to apologize in a way she would understand. It would be nice if he understood himself. Hell, he wasn't a kid anymore, but he'd come on to her like an oversexed teenager. He'd deliberately not given her a chance. He'd deliberately pushed all her buttons—and it had been so very easy, too easy. The look on her face had told him volumes about her marriage. She and Mr. Dynamite had shared sex, but not love-making. In contrast he was demanding everything from her every time they got close. No wonder she'd run.

The realization brought another more disturbing thought to mind. She'd said she loved him, but from what he'd seen and experienced earlier, it was quite possible she'd confused sex with love. Despite his actions, Hal knew he hadn't confused the two. He loved her all right, too much to let her muddle around alone with the feeling he'd dropped on her.

Locking the door behind him, he glanced up the street and saw her Mustang parked a block away. She hadn't gone home, but that was where he was going. He was through with private talks in public places. Physically and emotionally, he'd reached his limit on interruptions. His absolute limit.

Moving slowly, the wheels of Stevie's Mustang crunched on the gravel road winding through the trees to her cabin. The moon hung high in the night sky. The stars shone like diamond studs nested in black velvet. At the end of the driveway, Stevie pulled to a stop and lowered her head to the steering wheel. The two beers she'd nursed all night had done little to settle her nerves. If anything, she was more on edge now than when she'd run out on Hal.

A heavy sigh tightened her chest, adding to the ache he'd left, the one she hadn't been able to shake. She turned her head sideways and looked down the meadow, her gaze settling on his cabin. The presence of his truck told her he was home, probably asleep, alone in his big four-poster. Another sigh followed the first. She should have stayed in town at Nola's. Even being this close to him strained her resolve. She wanted him so badly.

So badly . . . Stevie caught her lower lip between her teeth and squeezed her eyes shut. *So badly*. She hurt all over with wanting him. The curve of her breast still held the warmth of his touch. Her mouth still felt the loving bruise of his kiss. She wanted to trace every line of his body with her hands and follow with her lips. She wanted to taste the sweet saltiness of his skin on her tongue. She wanted to hold him tight and tell him of her love while he . . .

"Damn," she whispered into the silence, realizing she was driving herself nuts. But the images remained strong and clear: Hal's sun-bronzed body pressing against hers; his muscular legs sliding around hers; a golden mane of hair falling over her face and brushing her cheeks as he kissed her again and again.

A wave of longing turned her next curse into a soft groan. She couldn't go on like this. She was bound to burn up. She had a choice to make, a decision, and she had to make it now, or suffer through another night of dreaming restless dreams and turning her bed into a battle zone of sleeplessness.

Hal had given her one set of alternatives—fight or make love—and Stevie knew she didn't have the energy for fighting. In her mind, though, she phrased the choices differently—take him or leave him.

Take him or leave him, Stevie. Decide. She

straightened her arms and slumped down in the
car, resting her head on the back of the seat. She
silently admitted she didn't have the energy for
leaving him. A month of working side by side
with him, a few stolen, searing kisses, and he'd
left an indelible mark on her untouchable heart.
She'd never been more confused in her life, or
more aware of a man. He invaded her mind with a
powerful ease, filling every niche and cranny, leaving her no peace and no place to go without him.

*Take him or . . . take him, Stevie. Take him
and take a chance.* Her eyes drifted across the
dark horizon and down the meadow to his cabin,
and as she gazed longingly at the small house, the
door opened.

Hal walked across the porch and leaned his
shoulder against one of the upright posts supporting the roof. His feet were bare, his shirt
unbuttoned to the waist where it was half-tucked
into his jeans. His hair was pushed back from his
face from the repeated, broad sweeps of his hands
running through it while he'd paced the floor.
He'd tried sleeping, but like every other night it
had been an exercise in futility. All he really wanted
was to be with Stevie. He wanted her with every
fiber of his being. He stared out over the moonlit
landscape and saw only wide gray eyes, a soft
mouth parted in anticipation, and the fullness of
her breasts cupped in his hands. He'd never been
crazy in love before, but he knew what he felt was
love and it was sure driving him crazy.

Frustration tightened his hand around the post
and lowered his chin to his chest. Maybe it was
time to leave the Trail. He had the tax money and
a little extra. And it was a rare night when he
didn't get another job offer. If he didn't work for

her, he knew he could catch up with her no matter how fast she ran.

But he'd promised to stay. He also knew that if he left, she'd be losing the best bartender she'd ever had, and all the money he brought in for her. From the way she'd been treating him, he'd figured his drawing power was the only reason she hadn't fired him. He was damned if he did, damned if he didn't. He'd been in some pretty tight spots before, but it had taken Stevie Lee to show him the true meaning of being between a rock and a hard place.

Where was she? The thought echoed through the emptiness in his heart. She should have been home by now. No, he quickly amended, she should have been with him. She should always be with him.

Stevie watched him, watched the moonlight caress the muscular curves of his chest and the dejected bend of his head, until she couldn't watch him anymore. Slowly she got out of the car, hesitating for a moment with her hand grasping the top of the door and one booted foot on the running board. She glanced once at her cabin, then down the meadow at Hal. What good was love if it wasn't shared? she asked herself, knowing the answer was "No good at all." Then she closed the car door and, step by step, followed her dreams down the pine-bordered path.

Hal's head lifted at the sound, and through the shadows of the night he saw her coming for him. His breath caught, but only for an instant, then started up again deep and slow. Moonlight dappled the trail of wildflowers and the long, slender curves of her body as she appeared and disappeared between the trees, tightening his heart with every stride. He held himself very still as he watched her. She had to come to him.

On the other hand, if she changed her mind and started back up the hill, he guaranteed she wouldn't get five feet. The truth brought a wry grin to his mouth, and that's how Stevie found him when she stepped up on the porch.

The smile alone was enough to shake her confidence, coupled with his silence she found herself coming to a stop far short of her initial destination. Suddenly she felt quite foolish. What had she had in mind? A seduction? Throwing herself at him? And all because she'd let her emotions override her common sense and had worked herself into a dither of hormones?

Yes, she admitted, she'd had all of those things in mind. Her hormones were still frenzied beneath what she hoped was a calm exterior. He still looked incredibly enticing: The hard flat planes of his abdomen tightly muscled, causing her fingers to curl into her palm; the length of flaxen hair swept off his face in those twin manelike arcs; the casual stance of his lanky body relaxed against the porch railing—and that midnight smile teasing his mouth and her imagination.

"Hi," she said softly.

"Hi, Stevie," his rough voice added a depth and richness to her name unlike any other's. "Nice night."

"Beautiful," she agreed.

Hal nodded, letting his gaze roam down her body. He noticed the subtle shifting of her weight from one foot to the other, the nervous tangling of her fingers through the ends of her hair, and the shy, downcast angle of her eyes. She'd come for him all right, and now that she had him, she wasn't quite sure what to do with him. Fortunately he didn't suffer from the same lack of ideas.

"Very beautiful. The most beautiful I've ever seen," he broke the moment of silence softly, and his voice lowered to a raspy drawl. "Do you want to come over here?"

With the slightest of gestures he reached out his hand to her. Even with his encouragement Stevie found her boots glued to the porch.

"It's been a long time," she choked the words out around the growing lump in her throat.

"For me too."

"I mean a very long time."

His grin broadened, flashing white in the darkness of his face. "I thing we can figure it out," he said, teasing, lifting his hand higher. "It's like riding a bike . . . only much, much better."

The first step was the hardest. The second and the third came easier, and when her fingers touched his, he took her hand and gently pulled her closer.

"No running away this time, Stevie," he said softly, the smile fading from his face.

She shook her head, sending a tumble of honey-brown hair sliding over her shoulders.

"No turning back." His eyes darkened with a serious light, reflecting the intensity of his need.

Once again she shook her head.

"Okay, then," he said with a sigh, leaning back against the railing. And slowly but surely, he reached out, removed her jacket, and began unbuttoning her shirt.

Eight

One by one, his fingers slipped the buttons through their holes, baring her skin to the cool night breeze. When the last button was released, he slid his hand inside her shirt and undid the front clasp of her bra.

Stevie felt the tremor of his fingers between her breasts, and then, ever so slowly, he pushed the soft pink cotton and wisps of satin to either side. The heavy ache she'd been fighting all night increased in intensity, winding down through her body and settling between her thighs. With just one touch, he had her back to the place where she'd been in his arms, breathless, wanting and waiting for more.

The moon made a silvery track across her creamy skin, lighting a path for his hand to follow. He caressed the ripe fullness of her breasts, felt the weight and softness of each, all the while wondering how he'd lasted this long without her.

"Stevie," he spoke her name gently, sliding his

hand up her chest and throat, tilting her chin so he could see into her eyes. They were wide and soft, dark and mysterious in the starlight, and they filled him with longing. "I've never been in love before, but I'm in love now. I don't know how it happened, or why, or what it all means . . . besides this"—with the slightest of pressures on the back of her neck, he drew her closer and buried his head in the silky veil of hair falling over her shoulder—"but I want to know, Stevie. I want you to teach me." His mouth opened over her ear, soft and wet, sending shock waves coursing over her body. "Teach me how to love you," he whispered. "How to make love to you."

Every word seared his message on her heart and lit a flame deep inside her. Delicately his tongue traced the outside of her ear. Gently his teeth gnawed a path along her jaw to her mouth.

"Teach me, Stevie." His breath warmed her lips. "And I'll teach you how to make love to me."

And so he began, taking her hands in his and showing her the softness of his skin and the hardness of the muscles beneath. The heated warmth of his body pressed against her breasts played a sensory counterpoint to the cooler air blowing across her face and shoulders. Stevie rubbed against him, her mouth finding the hollow curve of his collarbone, and felt his sharp intake of breath in the contraction of his chest. This was where she belonged, with her fantasies coming to life in her arms. Every touch, every kiss brought a response, urging her on to greater exploration of the wonder of Halsey Morgan.

He sighed when she traced the column of his throat with her tongue, his eyes drifting closed and his head falling back. His skin was salty and sweet, warm and exciting. He groaned when her fingers splayed across and lingered on the tightness of his abdomen. Touch for touch, his body met each foray of her hands, opened fully for her, exquisitely in tune with her desires.

The rest of the night flowed around them in an abundance of earth's nature and the universe's far-off lights. Darkness and wilderness surrounded them in a veil of privacy on the porch, leaving them free to find each other.

From the purity of the high Himalayas to the sultriness of a Calcutta night, Hal had discovered nothing to equal the magic silkiness of a half-naked Stevie Lee giving herself to him. She let him taste the textures of her skin, her hands rough from work, her breasts and throat tantalizing with their softness. She moaned her pleasure when he opened her jeans, and sighed deeply when he brought her against him.

Her hands tangled through the flaxen gold of his hair as she pulled his mouth down on hers, and with his kiss, slow and sweet, she felt herself melt inside. He was the man she needed, the love she'd been waiting for.

Hal felt her softening in his arms and held her closer, but it wasn't close enough. He was torn between taking her or continuing this gentle game of pleasure they were playing. He'd been without either for so long. He wanted everything, wanted her to tease him and touch him until he reached the edge, then bring him back down and start all over again—and he told her, in the lowest of whispers, his mouth moving across the curve of her brow.

"Ah, yes, Stevie," he said huskily as her fingers moved down the front of his jeans. "Yes." Instinct and desire guided her hand, and when she hesitated, Hal guided her again, showing her just the way he needed her, how much he wanted her.

He was bare beneath his pants, giving her free access to seek the muscled curves of his back, the tender planes of his hipbones, and the special softness of the skin at the tops of his thighs. Slowly her hands stroked inward, meeting to hold him with her palm and fingertips. She touched his arousal, and her breath caught in her throat, electrifying her emotions and quickening her pulse. This time, though, instead of sinking into desire, Stevie found herself lifting to meet him.

A trail of yearning kisses drew her higher even as Hal slid down the post and pulled her between his legs. Their bodies met, his nakedness against her lace, his rhythm matching hers in gentle surges. A tightening pleasure stretched them to the edge of control. His kisses became wilder and found a matching abandon in the erotic track of her tongue following his jaw to his ear—until he couldn't take anymore.

"Stevie?"

"Mmmm," she murmured.

He rose against her, cupping her face in his hands. "You feel so good, so right." His thumbs slowly traced the high curve of her cheeks, his skin rough and calloused against the satiny softness of hers. Passion-smudged eyes drifted closed under the gentleness of his touch. His mouth lowered for the lightest of kisses on her full, sweet mouth. "I love you, Stevie Lee. You're warm and wonderful and beautiful . . . and I love you." His breath whispered across her lips, and his voice lowered to a raspy drawl. "Come with me."

Stevie felt his hand slide down her arm and his fingers entwine with hers. Once was enough for his request. She willingly went with him inside the cabin, her head resting on his shoulder, her heart full of tenderness and desire.

A shaft of moonlight spilled through his bedroom window, laying across his rumpled sheets and quilts in silver and shadow. Without a word he shrugged out of his shirt, letting it fall to the floor as he reached for the pale pink cotton draped over her breasts. His hands slid over her shoulders, pushing the cloth away even as he pulled her against his chest.

Her shirt joined his, and after a long searching kiss, the rest of their clothes followed, piece by piece until he held her naked in his arms. Stevie's breath quickened under the lazy track of his mouth up the side of her neck, the heated caresses of his hands down the length of her back.

"Hal," she sighed the name of her love, feeling his body come alive against hers. "You, too, are so very beautiful"—with the backs of her fingers she stroked the taut planes of his abdomen—"when I touch you here, and here . . ." her voice broke softly with the ache of wanting.

Hal understood every nuance of her emotions. They pulsed through him in waves as his mouth stole the rest of her words. The tension and excitement she created needed no more explanation than the riot of his senses, the craving in his soul to be one with her.

In the echoing passion of her kiss, he found the answers to love. In the arching of her body against his, he found the answers to loneliness. And touch by touch he gave everything he found back to her.

The muscles in his arms tightened with the strength to carry her to the bed and to hold her beneath him and to love her completely, slowly, and languorously while her satin soft thighs wrapped around his waist. He never wanted to stop, he wanted to be inside her forever.

"Stevie . . . open your eyes."

Her response revealed dove-gray eyes darkened by passion and need, shadowed by sooty lashes.

"Ah, yes." He groaned, feeling her draw him deeper and higher.

The action came naturally, easily, almost desperately, and suddenly she was entering unexplored territory inside of herself, new levels of sensation she hadn't thought existed.

Hal saw the wonder widen her eyes, and the barest of smiles played at the corner of his mouth.

"Hal, I never . . ." she said with a gasp.

"Shh," he reassured her softly, kissing her mouth, the side of her nose, the curve of her brow. "Take your time. I'm not going anywhere without you . . . not tonight . . . not tonight, Stevie." His words picked up the cadence of his body, turning his whispers into an aural assault on her senses. From every quarter he plied her with the sights, sounds, and physical pleasures of his love.

Stevie felt the world slip farther and farther away, leaving her with only one crucial realm of awareness—Halsey Morgan. Indigo eyes held hers with a sultry gleam. Soft, golden hair brushed across her skin. Strong arms and hands flexed around her and caressed her, always pulling her closer. He left no part of her untouched, from the sentient layer of her skin to the deepest recesses

of her heart. He loved her forever, as he'd promised, until the lines between her thoughts and
feelings, the differences between thinking and
touching, vanished into the fantasy of her wildest
dreams. Wave after wave of the purest pleasure
coursed through her body, binding her to him
more tightly than their entwined limbs.

For long moments afterward, he continued to
kiss her, each touch of his lips gentler than the
one before, and ever so slowly Stevie felt the tension leave his body and a new peace overcome
them both.

"Ah, Stevie, you are so sweet." He sighed in her
ear, his fingers brushing sweat-dampened tendrils of hair away from her face. "So very sweet. I
needed to love you a long time ago."

She replied silently with a trail of soft wet kisses
along his throat. Even sated with pleasure, she
couldn't get enough of him. The weight of him
pressing her into the bed gave her a tranquil
sense of security. The overheated, masculine scent
of him surrounded her in a veil of private sensuality.

Free from common sense restraints and the frantic urges of desire, she allowed her mouth and
hands to leisurely explore every hardened curve of
his body: The broadness of his shoulders, the
corded strength of his arms, the sun-browned
satin quality of his skin.

Hal stretched under her stroking, tightening
and releasing each muscle in turn as her slender
fingers kneaded his body. "Mmm, that feels good."

"Sure does," she said, sighing. With the back of
her hand she traced the angle of his jaw up to the
shaggy mane of his hair, reveling in the closeness
they shared. A year of marriage had given her

nothing in comparison, nothing except betrayal, a measure of heartache, and an inadequate idea of the pleasure to be found with a man. But she'd found it with this man whom she'd so easily discounted as a mere detail in her desire to make a good deal on his property.

The thought brought with it an instant, overwhelming sense of guilt and dropped a shadow over her happiness. His lovemaking had left her emotionally vulnerable, too vulnerable to hide from her own selfish, heartless motives. *Bad news, Stevie. Halsey Morgan is alive . . . Sure he follows his own star—right off the edge of the earth . . . Pukapuka? Bora Bora? What does it matter? They say it's his boat all right.*

The memories brought a stark realization crashing down on top of her guilt. She might have lost him. If he'd died, she'd have seventy thousand dollars in her hands instead of the warm, powerful body she held so closely. The thought scared her senseless.

"Hal—" her voice caught on a broken whisper. "You could have died!"

His hand stopped in mid-caress, and a pair of quizzically wary blue eyes slowly lifted to meet hers. "Just now, you mean?"

"On the boat!"

"Oh, that." Visible relief brought a quick grin to his mouth. "Not really, Stevie. I would have had to work at it." He dismissed her fears with a shrug and went back to enjoying the beauty and softness of her body.

"Hal, I mean it. You might not have come back."

"I always come back," he said easily, reaching up and brushing his thumb across her cheek. "Sometimes it just takes longer than others."

"But—"

"No buts about it. I always come back—always," he repeated for her sake, feeling her distress and wondering what had brought it on. He didn't have to wait long to find out.

"I'm sorry, Hal. I've been selfish and awful. All the time you were suffering on that island I wasn't even thinking of you. Only of myself and all the money I'd make"—a small, choking sob broke through on a gasp—"and not once did I think of you and what you were going through. I didn't even think of you as a person, just a meal ticket out of here. And now I'm . . . I'm . . ."

"Stevie, Stevie." He drew his fingertip across her lower lip, effectively silencing her with his touch. "Hey, come on now. You didn't even know me. And believe me, if I'd known you, I'd have been working a lot harder to get back here."

"You could have died," she said, her voice full of sorrow, her eyes wide and filling with tears.

What she said was true, as Hal knew only too well, but faced with her sadness he decided to gloss over the bare facts. Because, quite honestly, he didn't understand why she was being so hard on herself. He'd certainly run into rougher characters, people who had had real and dangerous designs on his continued existence. In contrast sweet Stevie Lee filled his life with more love than he'd ever expected to find. She easily deserved the best of him.

"Stevie, I hate to disappoint you, but being stranded in the South Pacific wasn't all that bad," he said with a smooth smile crooking one side of his mouth. "Delilah was a little rough on me, but the island . . . ah, darlin', she was paradise. Palm trees swaying over the beaches. Sunsets that went to the end of the world. I had enough of *Freedom* left to supply myself with the basics, and the ocean came up with a few luxuries every now and then. If you'd been there, it would have been perfect." There, he thought, that's pretty much the whole story in a nutshell, without the gory details but also without any lies.

Stevie listened to every word, imagining the paradise he described as she absently wiped the moisture off her cheeks. When he finished, she asked, "Exactly how much of your boat did you have left?" She remembered clearly the stories about the wooden planks washing up in French Polynesia, the ones supposedly belonging to his boat.

Stifling a sigh, Hal glanced up to a point somewhere beyond those curious gray eyes and weighed the question in his mind. He tried it one way, then another, and still didn't come up with a way to disguise the facts.

"About half," he finally admitted.

His answer was met with silence, then a soft screech. "*Half?*"

"Yeah. But it was the big half."

"*Half?*"

"It was definitely the big half. A really huge half now that I think about it. I had the whole bow, most of port, and a good section of starboard. Mostly I was missing a shave or two off the stern. If I hadn't lost the mast, there's no telling how long I could have held out."

Growing up on a lake in the middle of the Rocky Mountains was a little different than growing up on a lake anyplace else. It didn't necessarily result in nautical knowledge, but even Stevie knew that what he'd described was a disaster of the highest magnitude.

"What happened to the mast?" she asked quietly in her best no-nonsense tone.

Hal knew when he was beaten. But her tears had stopped, so he figured he hadn't done too badly. "Well, I'll tell you," he began, easing his weight off of her and settling himself on his side. "For as much as I paid for the damn thing, you'd think it could have withstood more than a few hours of better than average winds."

"Better than average?" she inquired, questioning his description with a lift of one silky eyebrow.

"Better than average, a notch or two above gale, but definitely a notch below hurricane strength."

"I see."

Hal completely missed the note of reproach in her two-word statement, concentrating instead on his own interpretation. "I wish you could have, Stevie. That storm was the wildest thing I've ever tangled with in my whole life. I knew the seas in that area were prone to monster storms, but the route was kind of a shortcut, and it wasn't monster storm season." He chuckled. "Old Delilah, though, she didn't care what season it was. Man, she sucked me up and spit me out again and again and again. She ripped the shirt right off my back. She snapped my mast like a toothpick. A toothpick!" His eyes widened in awe. "I tell you, watching it career over *Freedom's* starboard beam just about did me in. I thought for sure I'd bought my last ticket on Mother Nature's wheel of fortune."

"In other words, you almost died."

"Almost," he agreed sheepishly, coming back from his memories. "But almost dying is like being a little bit pregnant. You either is, or you ain't . . . and I wasn't. When I came to on the beach, I still had all my pieces. Most of them were black and blue, and green and yellow, but they were all in working order. It was a helluva ride, though."

"Oh, Hal," his name was a sigh from her lips. "What am I going to do with you?"

"If you're short of ideas, I've got a couple I think we can pull off." A sly grin teased his mouth and warmed the depths of his eyes.

"I'm serious."

"So am I," his voice lowered to a rough drawl as he pulled her over on top of him. "Real serious."

Stevie snuggled up closer, wanting and needing to feel the warmth of him, the life in him. "I don't want you to change, Halsey Morgan. But I don't want to lose you either."

"Stevie—"

"Just promise me this," she interrupted him softly. She was unsure of what she was about to say, but in her heart she knew she had to say it. "Promise me, Hal, that as long as we're together, for as long as you want me, you won't go off and die somewhere."

"I can't." His arms tightened around her before she could move. "Because as long as I draw breath, I'll want you. And, Stevie, no matter how hard I try, sooner or later I'm going to die." His grin flickered back to life. "If it's any consolation, I haven't survived this long just by luck. Over the years I've acquired a few skills that keep me landing on my feet, and I never give a place a second shot at me. Mount Everest, the old goddess mother of the world, has seen the last of me. She held on too tight last time. The same goes for one-man voyages across the South Pacific. I may be kind of wild, but I'm no fool."

"Me either." He felt the answering warmth of her smile touch him like the sun. "I know a good thing when it hits me in the face . . . and Hal?" —she lowered herself on his body, her mouth coming close to his—"You're the best."

Hal's smile slowly faded under the intensity of emotion reflected in her eyes. Her hair, loosened by their lovemaking, flowed over her shoulders and fanned across his chest. Moonlight graced her breasts with a pearly hue. His eyes drank in the exquisitely feminine form in his arms, and slowly, but inevitably, he found himself wanting her again. Without a word, he reached up and slid his hand through the tangle of honey-brown hair streaming down her back.

Stevie's breath caught at the familiar pressure between her thighs and the warm, lambent light darkening his eyes. A tender ache grew between them as he held her captive with his gaze. And then once again, Halsey Morgan—adventurer extraordinaire—transported her to the land of enchantment.

"This was a great idea." Hal levered himself up on the hood of the Mustang and handed her the beer he'd gotten out of the cooler in the trunk. On a rare night when neither of them worked, they'd decided to cruise up to the summit of Trail Ridge Road, the highest continuously paved road on the continent. More than an hour had gone by since the last car had passed.

"I love it up here at night. The stars so close, you can touch them. No one else is around." Stevie leaned back on the windshield. "I feel like I'm on top of the world—and I own it all."

Hal nodded silently in agreement, looking out over the mountain ranges piling up on each other as far as the eye could see. Longs Peak, the Gore Range, the Never Summers, they brought back good memories of other mountains, even higher and wilder. A very familiar wistfulness caught at his heart. He'd been grounded for two months now, and even though the one he'd spent loving Stevie Lee had been the most incredible in his life, he was starting to get itchy feet.

"Have you ever done any technical climbing?" he asked, glancing over his shoulder.

"I've been to the top of Longs a couple of times, but we hiked it. I've never done any rope work."

"Longs is about fourteen thousand feet, isn't it?"

"Fourteen thousand, two hundred, and fifty-six, and I felt every one of them," she said with a teasing groan.

"But you didn't have any trouble? No altitude sickness?" An idea had taken hold in his mind, a stopgap measure at best, but maybe enough to take the edge off his wanderlust.

"Darlin'," she said in an exaggerated drawl, giving him a wry glance. "You're talking to a lady born at ten thousand feet. It's going to take more than another four or five to do me in."

"Well, darlin', how about another fourteen?" He scooted up on the hood and laid sideways on the windshield to face her. He rested his head in his hand.

Big gray eyes studied him for a moment, then she said, "As far as I know, the closest eight thousand meter peak is about two thousand dollars away. And if I had enough money to get that far, climbing mountains wouldn't exactly be at the top of my itinerary—no pun intended."

"No pun accepted." He grinned. "Okay, so we won't be mounting an assault on Everest this summer. How about doing Long's Peak with me and a few yards of rope?"

"Not that stuff you use to tie your truck together?"

His grin broadened to encompass his whole face. "No, I've got some real good stuff I keep under the bed."

He'd given her the perfect line, and Stevie couldn't resist. Cuddling up closer, she arched forward and whispered in his ear, "You keep some pretty good stuff on top of the bed too."

Her sultry voiced compliment went through him right to the core, starting an instant spiral of pleasure in his loins. With one smooth move, he rolled her over on top of him and let her feel the heat she'd initiated. A slow, suggestive smile replaced his easy grin. "You're pure trouble, Stevie Lee. Sweet and pure trouble."

"You seem to be handling it," she said, pressing herself against him and tangling her fingers through the silver-gold hair framing his face.

"Do you want to talk about mountains"—her next move made him catch his breath, turning it into a soft moan—"or get naked in the backseat?"

"The backseat is a little small."

"Trust me. We won't need much room," he promised, his hands tightening on the small of her back, his hips moving to meet her halfway.

Darkening blue eyes held her mesmerized as each minute of budding pleasure moved into the next, until her arms weakened and she fell against him. Her head nestled into the curve of his shoulder.

"When do you want to climb Long's Peak?" she whispered, not missing a beat of his passionate rhythm.

"Anytime after we make love. Come on, I'll race you to the backseat."

Holding her close in his arms, he slowly slid off the hood, and inch by playful, teasing inch they worked themselves into the car.

Nine

Stevie limped to the next table and set her tray down with a thump. Every bone in her body ached, but she had no regrets. Standing on top of Long's Peak with Hal had been worth every bruise and scrape, and it had whetted her appetite for more. She doubted if she'd ever be ready for Everest, but that still left a whole world to explore. They were starting in again next week with a white-water rafting trip down the Colorado.

With a groan she lifted the full tray and headed back to the bar. Day by day he was showing her the beauty of her own backyard, expanding her horizons beyond the Trail's End, and making her dreams come alive. Certainly Trail Ridge Road would never look the same to her again.

A small smile tweaked a corner of her mouth at the memory. She'd always wondered how people ended up naked in the backseat of a car—and now she knew. It was easy, really easy, with a man like Halsey Morgan. To Hal, making love came as naturally as breathing. He didn't need candle-light, wine, and flowers to create romance. He did it with his mind and body, anyplace, anytime. Her smile softened, her expression became dreamy. Long's Peak would never look the same again either. And considering the lack of oxygen up there, maybe he didn't even need to breathe to make love.

Hal watched her weave her way through the tables with the special smile on her face, and he knew exactly what she was thinking about. He'd never met a woman like Stevie Lee. Hanging from the rope, she'd trusted him implictly, enjoying every moment. She was the same way when they made love, so giving and open. Somehow when his life had been at an all-time low, he'd walked into a shabby little bar in a backwater town and found the love of his life. Maybe Delilah hadn't done so badly for him after all.

"A whiskey sour and a scotch, please," a construction worker named Quade requested for himself and his wife. The two of them had been slow dancing all night to the songs on the jukebox, regardless of the fact that the Trail didn't have a dance floor. Hal admired their ability to make do with what they had; for he knew if he wasn't stuck behind the bar, he'd be shuffling through the tables right along with them, Stevie in his arms, oblivious to the rest of the folks. Love did crazy things to a man.

Mixing the drinks with a natural ease, he kept one eye on his lady. He wondered if she knew how beautiful she was; if she knew what happened to him deep inside every time he looked at her. It was happening to him now—a filling up of his heart, a longing to reach out and touch her. He'd tell her again tonight as he'd told her every night. And as she'd done every night, she'd wrap him in her love.

"Stevie, please go home. I'll close up," he offered again as she dropped off her tray and slid onto the stool at the end of the bar.

"Oh, Hal," she said, lowering her head to a resting spot in the cradle of her arms. "You've already let me go home early three times this week. It's your turn. Besides, I can't afford to keep you on the clock."

"I haven't been on the clock this week," he informed her with a knowing look.

"I've been keeping track in my head. You're up to forty-two hours so far"—she lifted a hand to stop his protest—"and you'll get paid for every one."

"Stevie, I'm pulling five hundred a week out of here on tips alone. I should be paying you."

"You wouldn't make much of a union man," she teased with a soft smile.

"You go home and warm up the bed, and we'll call it even."

"Which bed?" she asked around a big yawn.

"You're opening tomorrow, so let's make it your place."

"Good idea." The mind was willing, but the body refused to budge. Letting her legs dangle, she snuggled up closer on the bar. "I'll leave in a minute."

She'd no sooner closed her eyes, than a name from the past popped them wide open again.

"Hey, Kip!" A man hollered out as the front door opened.

With a mixture of weariness and dismay, she watched as six feet two inches of predictably unpredictable ex-husband walked into the Trail. Why, oh, why, she started to ask herself, then stopped. She knew why he'd come—for the same reason he always came.

"TNT! I thought you were in Steamboat Springs," another customer called cheerily.

Personally Hal didn't know what to think. In the rare moments when he'd thought about Kip Brown, he hadn't imagined such a clean-cut, good-looking boy. Sleazy, maybe; older, definitely—but not this youthful replica of the Marlboro Man. He wondered if the kid knew he could damage himself by wearing his jeans so tight. Glancing at Stevie, he looked for a clue to what she was feeling, but the mild furrowing of her brow didn't give him much to go on.

"Hi, Kip. You're looking great," a lady in the corner said, irking Hal to the core.

"Chuck, Darlene." He lifted a hand in greeting and graced the couple with a dazzling smile. "What's happening, Eddie?"

"Not a helluva lot since you left. Town's gotten kinda slow."

"Ah, come on, Eddie. I can't believe that. I left you Stevie, didn't I?" He grinned, and slapped the older man on the back.

Now there's a clue, Hal thought, his jaw tightening. When the situation called for it, he'd been known to blow enough smoke to cloud any issue, but he'd never heard anything like the crass line Mr. Dynamite had just delivered. He thought about yelling out "Yeah, you left her, so take a hike, kid." He thought about going over the bar—something Stevie had told him never to do—and tossing the jerk out on his butt. The increasingly pained look on her face kept him from doing either. He'd let her handle the situation her way. He'd let her cut Kip Brown down to size; she deserved the first shot.

So he stood his ground by the cash register, strangling a beer mug and feeling incredibly territorial and ready for a quick fight.

Stevie wished she'd left the first time Hal had asked. Darlene was right. Kip did look great, but then looking great was his strong point. Sandy brown hair swept back from a face born to break hearts. Thick, black lashes framed a pair of liquid brown eyes, and an ever-present grin played around his mouth. As usual he wore his clothes with a casual grace. Expensive jeans faded by the factory to a dove-gray molded his long legs and lean hips, and matched his cowboy boots. A crisp, white cotton shirt with a famous logo on the pocket fit across his broad shoulders and chest like a glove. Even when they'd been struggling along together, Kip had always managed to look like he owned the whole town. Knowing his precarious financial position, she wondered how he did it.

"Hi, sweetness. How's my girl?" He stopped less than a foot away from her, and leaned forward on the bar, all smiles and mischief.

Come on Stevie, Hal silently urged, let him have it.

"Fine."

Fine? Both of Hal's eyebrows rose slightly. *Fine?*

"Well, you're sure looking good. How's Tiva?"

"Staying out of trouble. Blue had puppies again, five this time."

"I told your dad a thousand times to get her spayed. She's a regular puppy machine. I saw the Mustang out front. Is she holding up all right?"

"Still beats anything on four wheels in the county."

"Good girl. If you take care of her, you'll get your money back just like I told you. Don't let anybody except Doug under the hood. The kid has magic fingers with an engine."

Doug? The mechanical disaster of the free world? Hal's jaw went slack. What was going on here? Where was the lady who'd run him ragged for a month?

"You know, Stevie," he continued in a more intimate tone, "I've really missed you."

Hal's control snapped. "Wait a minute, cowboy," his tone gave the term a derogatory slant. "I don't know who in the—"

"Who's this guy?" Kip asked Stevie.

"He's—" she started, but Hal didn't give her a chance.

"I'm the guy who's picking up all the pieces you left: I tune the Mustang; I fix the beer coolers when they break; I keep the suppliers off Stevie's back." Hal slowly leaned forward, resting both hands on the bar and leveling a steely-eyed glare at the younger man. "And I'm the guy she comes home to every night. Got it?"

Kip nodded. "Got it."

"Good." At least that's what he said, but somehow he got the feeling he hadn't made that much of an impression on her ex-husband. The man certainly didn't look worried.

"You must be Halsey Morgan," he said, pushing his Stetson farther back on his head. "I heard you were taking good care of Stevie. Kong says he hasn't been right in the head since you hit him."

"I only hit him once," Hal said, trying another thinly veiled threat.

"Must have been a helluva punch." The kid grinned.

Hal gave up. Kip Brown was so laid-back, it was no wonder why nobody hated him. "Do you want a beer?" he asked carefully, a part of him still expecting a show of spirit.

"Please."

"That's a buck seventy-five," Stevie said calmly.

Hal shot her a surprised glance. She was serious. She hadn't budged from her resting place on the bar, but her mouth had a definite no-nonsense set and her eyes were glacial gray. Between them they probably gave away ten drinks a night—but not to Kip Brown, not even a lousy glass of draft. His own spirits picked up considerably.

"Ah, Stevie. It's just a beer," Kip said.

"To you it's just a beer. To me it's a buck seventy-five of product. I can't have you stealing me blind on both ends, Kip. I'll never make it." Her voice remained mellow, almost to the point of boredom, and Hal realized he was witnessing a scene the two of them had played many times before.

"Can we talk about this in the back room?" Kip asked, and Hal noted the first note of uncertainty in the other man's manner.

"Sure." Stevie shrugged and slid off the stool.

With a grin and tip of his hat, Kip followed her around the end of the bar. Hal was okay with the turn of events, until out of the corner of his eye he caught the gentle pat of the cowboy's hand on Stevie's rear end.

Instant dislike welled up in his chest. The kid was smooth, damn smooth. If he got any smoother, he was going to be peeling his butt off the boardwalk.

Stevie moseyed over to her office chair and

plopped herself down. Kip leaned his hip against the desk, his glance straying to the open ledger.

"I'm in trouble."

"So what else is new?"

"I mean really in trouble this time, Stevie." He pushed off the desk and began pacing the room. Not once did he meet her gaze. "I have to have my cash now. It's not as if you don't owe me. The divorce laid it out real clear. We had ten grand in this place—five belongs to me. You've paid me one—that leaves four."

"I can add," she said dryly. "But that doesn't mean I've got it. Besides, the deal says installments of five hundred. Not four grand flat out."

"I gave you the car."

"I'm still paying on it."

"I gave you the house."

"I'm still paying on it too."

"Brenda's pregnant."

"What?"

"She's pregnant, Stevie. I'm going to be a father." He stopped halfway across the office and looked up at her from under the brim of his hat, a sheepish grin curving his mouth.

She gasped. "A father? You?" Suddenly she was wide-awake.

"Pretty wild, huh?"

"Unbelievable," she agreed breathlessly. "You're going to marry her, aren't you?"

"Next week. I was going to invite you, but Brenda didn't think it was a good idea."

"Well, thank God one of you is thinking!" Stevie choked back her shock.

Her tactlessness didn't go unnoticed, and slowly the smile faded from his mouth. "You never thought that much of me, did you, Stevie?"

"Kip, I—I loved you," she stammered, completely taken aback by his out-of-character statement. Talking about anything personal from down deep had never been their forte. "I still care about you."

"Yeah, the way you care about Doug and your mom, or Nola, but not the way you need to care about a husband. You never needed me, period." His voice lowered to a rough edge. "It took me a long time to figure that out, Stevie."

"I needed you," she said a bit more defensively, thoroughly confused by his new approach. "We started this business, didn't we?"

"You've missed the point, sweetheart," he said. "I'm talking about love and respect, and as usual you're talking about bottom lines and cash on the barrel. I didn't make much of a business partner for you either, did I?"

For a man whom she'd known most of her life, Kip was making her strangely uneasy. They were on the verge of some very deep truths, something they'd never come close to in their marriage. Stevie didn't see a need to dredge up the past now. "I couldn't have done it on my own."

"Wouldn't have done it is more likely."

"Well, maybe you're right there," she reluctantly conceded. "I can think of a hundred other things I'd rather do every day besides come down here and pour beer."

"And I can't think of anything else I'd rather do."

He was heading somewhere with this conversation; Stevie just knew it. "What are you getting at?"

He took his time in answering, settling himself on an empty case and resting his arm on the desk top. When he was situated, he looked her straight in the eye. "I want the Trail back. For once in my life I've got something worth fighting for—my family. I want to do right by them, Stevie. I don't want my kid growing up with just a bartender for a father. For four grand I can buy my way into the bar where I work in Steamboat, but they're only talking five percent of the business. I'd rather have my own place, this place. I know I can make a good living from this bar."

Stevie slumped back in her chair with a sense of wonderment and delight. Against all odds Kip 'TNT' Brown finally had grown up. "Where will you get the money to buy me out?"

"Brenda." When Stevie stared quizzically at him, he added quickly, "She has a trust fund and she wants a clean break. Six thousand dollars, Stevie. Think what you can do with it."

What were they doing back there? Hal wondered for the thousandth time. He tried to resist checking the clock again, but his eyes lifted upward anyway. Forty minutes. He'd had her back there for forty minutes. When he thought about all the things he could have done with her in forty minutes, he felt a little queasy. She was putty in that back room. *With you, not her ex-husband. Ex-husband!*

Hal took a deep calming breath, which didn't calm him in the least. One way or the other, Stevie Lee was going to be the death of him.

"Hal? I think you gave me the wrong drink," a man quietly suggested, pushing his glass over the bar.

"What did you order, Ned?"

"Gin and tonic."

Hal took a sip and set the glass down. "This is a scotch and soda," he explained absently, and went back to polishing the finish off the cash register. What *were* they doing back there?

Ned started to say something, then changed his mind and wandered away with the drink.

"Promise me you'll think about it and get back to me?" Kip asked, walking Stevie back through the hallway with his arm around her shoulders.

"I promise." She smiled up at him. "I'm very happy for you."

"Thanks. You know, there's . . . uh . . . something else I came here to say tonight." He stopped just short of the bar and turned her in his arms. With visible effort, his dark brown eyes lifted to meet hers. "I always hated myself for running around on you, Stevie. I was serious when I said it took me a long time to figure out why I did it. I needed somebody to need me, to depend on me. You never did, and I can't blame you for that. I wasn't all that dependable back then."

"You weren't all that bad either. It takes two to make a marriage, and two to break one." A month ago Stevie would have choked on the words she spoke as truth tonight.

"That's mighty generous of you, ma'am," he said, giving her a big hug. With his arms around her and his mouth close to her ear, he whispered, "You're a good lady, Stevie, a strong lady. No regrets?"

"No regrets."

He squeezed her tightly for a long moment, then set her away. "If I want to get out of here with my face in one piece, I better leave now." He nodded toward the bar and the blond adventurer watching them with grim, steely blue eyes. "I've heard a lot about that guy. I think you may have met your match this time."

"I know I have," she admitted with a grin.

"Halsey. Nice meeting you." He tipped his hat on the way out, keeping well to the end of the bar.

Stevie watched him leave with a new lightness in her heart. Her gaze roamed over the bar, and for the first time she saw the place as an asset instead of a liability. With the mere scrawl of her signature, she could walk away with six thousand dollars. It had been Kip's dream, his talent that had breathed life into Trail's End. Only Hal's presence this summer had enabled her to even come close to running in the black.

As if on cue, her gaze met his. His eyes were still stormy behind the cool facade of his rugged face. When his hair swept back from his face, it wasn't because a stylist had spent hours getting it just so. No distinguishing label of any kind graced his shirt pockets. The wear on his jeans had been hard won, and his boots were made for walking—miles and years of it, up mountains, through rivers, across deserts.

Days in the sun and nights in the wild had lent a hardness to his body and put those wonderful feathery lines at the corners of his eyes. She doubted if his hair would ever find its natural color, or if his skin would ever lose its special golden luster. *Freedom*, he'd called his sailboat. He was the essence of freedom. Tonight, Kip had handed her her own freedom on a silver platter.

Hal forced himself to hold his painfully casual stance leaning against the low shelf behind the bar. Sometimes no matter how hard he tried, he couldn't tell what was going on in her mind. With time he hoped to figure her out completely, but the look of excitement Kip's visit had left in her eyes made him wonder if he'd get the chance.

"Good-looking kid," he said for starters.

"Takes after his mother."

"Dresses sharp," he lied, not really liking the put-together look but curious about what Stevie liked.

"If you like drugstore cowboys." She shrugged. "I never did figure out how he afforded such expensive clothes. I guess it's a matter of priorities. Mine were always on paying the bills."

"Yeah, I'm not much of a clotheshorse myself." The beginnings of a smile twitched a corner of his mouth.

"I noticed. But then,"—one winged brow lifted suggestively—"it's not exactly your clothes I'm interested in."

"Must be my money."

"Not exactly."

"My mind?" He pushed off the shelf and started walking toward her.

"Oh, you've got a fine mind, Mr. Halsey Morgan," she said with a sly smile, taking a step backward and leading him into the hall. "But I was thinking of something a little more . . . physical."

"Are you making a pass at me?" He followed her every move, slowly and surely closing the distance between them.

"For all practical purposes, yes."

His arms went around her the instant they touched, and he lowered his head to the curve of her shoulder. "I love you, Stevie Lee. I truly do. More than I've ever loved anyone else in my life."

The tender moves of his mouth on her neck sent a cascade of feelings down her body, turning her soft and warm inside. "Let's close this pop stand and go home together," she whispered, turning her lips to his ear.

"Shut down early?" Surprise registered in his husky voice. "I know we don't have much of a crowd, but I'm sure I can squeeze another fifty bucks out of them." What was he saying? He mentally kicked himself.

"Not tonight, Hal. I need you." She paused for a second as the reality of what she'd said hit home. Kip had been right; she'd never needed him. But this man, the one she held so dearly in her arms, she needed him the way the earth needs the sun.

Ten

Midmorning shadows hovered in the corners of Stevie's bedroom loft, turning the light a soft bluish-gray. Never an early riser, she considered the lack of an east-facing window a blessing. Hal, on the other hand, got up with the sun whether he could see it or not, no matter how late he'd stayed up the night before. Worse, he always was cheerful and full of energy the minute he opened his eyes.

Even through the protection of the pillow jammed around her head, Stevie heard him rattling around downstairs in the kitchen, singing to the radio and, more than likely, making his own brand of claptrap. Behind his back she'd taken to dumping a couple of heaping teaspoons of instant coffee into his lighthearted brew. She needed coffee with a power punch to start her system in the morning.

"Coffee's ready!" he hollered up from the bottom of the stairs.

"Hah," she whispered doubtfully, snuggling deeper into the bed.

"Come on, lady, get it in gear. I know you're awake up there, and you've got exactly . . ." he paused, and Stevie groaned, knowing what to expect next—"fifty-three minutes and forty-two seconds. Forty-one. Forty. Thirty-nine."

"All right, already," she said softly, hanging one leg over the bed. At his count of twenty-two, she hung the other leg over. The man was relentless; he never gave up on her, and he always got what he wanted.

At ten seconds and counting, she decided to give him a break and called down, "I'm up. I'm up."

"I'll believe it when I see it."

"Okay, Attila," she muttered under her breath, thrashing around in the covers until they released her. On leaden feet, she dragged herself to the top of the stairs. Grouchy, rumpled, and indignant, she peered down at him. "Satisfied?"

"Not when you look like that," he said, his gaze taking a leisurely tour up the creamy length of her legs to the high-cut teddy wrapping her body in soft cotton and lace. Loose, white ribbons trailed down the front of the lingerie, tangling up in the unbound strands of her hair. Until he'd met Stevie, he hadn't known such teasing concoctions existed, but with her he was making up for lost time. She had every color and style imaginable, and she wore them all with a sizzling, unconscious sensuality. No wonder she didn't have anything but jeans, T-shirts, and sweaters to wear over them. The lady must have spent a fortune, and by his estimation she'd spent it wisely. Watching her, Hal felt the heat building in his loins. He felt every breath she took, every rise and fall of her breasts shoot right through him, and he started up the stairs.

The predatory gleam in his eyes did more to wake Stevie up than any amount of verbal coercion. A very feminine tremor of apprehension wound its way into her anticipation, adding a sharp edge to the feelings tumbling through her body.

"Hal"—she edged away from the stairs, even as a soft smile curved her lips—"I don't think we have time for what you're thinking."

"Believe me, Stevie, what I've got in mind isn't going to take long." He kept on coming, one step at a time, an equally soft smile playing with the corners of his mouth. "You'll be surprised."

"Changing your style?" she inquired with a lift of one silky eyebrow.

"Just keeping you guessing." Two steps below her, he slid his arm around her thigh and still kept coming, lifting her onto his shoulder.

"Hal!" she said with a gasp, and gasped again as his open mouth traced the edge of her teddy over the curve of her hip. His wet, gnawing kisses never stopped. They traveled up her body as he lowered her to the bed. They teased the tops of her breasts and the valley between. His fingers unlaced her ribbons, inch by inch, slipping the lingerie from her body. And when he had her breathless and bare beneath him, he slid out of his jeans and into her.

The gentle force of him caught at her desire, carrying her instantly into a higher plane of sensation. Hal's head dropped to the curve of her neck as her tightening response drew a low groan from deep in his throat.

"Ah yes, Stevie, yes." His mouth came down hard on hers, devouring the sweet depths in an act of passion to match the rhythm of their bodies.

A whirlwind of the purest physical pleasure spiraled up from their joining, pushing her over the brink into a mindless realm where the only thing she felt was the man on top of her, around her, inside of her.

Long, sweet moments later, he lifted his head and rubbed his nose down the side of hers. "I think we set a new record," he whispered tenderly, kissing the side of her mouth.

Stevie's lashes fluttered open, her body still pulsing with the aftermath of climax. "Mmm," she agreed with her last ounce of energy, stretching languorously beneath him.

"I'll race you to the shower."

"You go ahead without me," she murmured, her eyes closing again for the drift back into sleep.

It was a short drift. "No way, lady"—he rolled her over on top of him—"we're up for good."

"Five minutes," she pleaded.

"I already gave you ten." A teasing grin spread across his face.

He had her there, and with reluctance apparent in every move, she forced herself to her feet. "Okay, but I get the shower."

"I'll bring your coffee in," he offered, bouncing up beside her.

"Thanks. That'll be . . . uh . . . wonderful," she said, but as he passed her, she privately cast her eyes toward the ceiling.

Hunched over the kitchen table, Stevie nursed

her first cup of real coffee while Hal was in the shower. The steam rose around her face, rich and aromatic. The cup warmed both of her hands. Her chin was nestled into the turned up collar of her sweater, and with very little effort she was sliding back toward oblivion. Consciousness never came before the second cup of mud—unless, of course, someone named Halsey Morgan wanted to make love.

"You know, Stevie,"—he appeared in the doorway, his hair wet and tousled, her black kimono wrapped around him—"you can go around the world on six thousand dollars. And in certain circles, you can go around two times on that kind of money."

"Great," she murmured, travel being at the bottom of her priority list at the moment. They'd discussed Kip's offer into the wee hours, Hal all gung ho and Stevie strangely reticent. She'd dreamed of a chance like the one Kip had given her, but now that she had it she was full of doubts. What would she do when the money was gone? What direction would her life take if she no longer had the Trail to run? Unlike Hal, she still had a mortgage and car payments. And for all her high flying dreams, she'd never actually stepped out of the borders of Colorado. The reality of leaving was a far sight different than sitting around flipping through books and travel brochures, and it scared her more than just a little bit.

"I'm serious," he continued as he moved around the kitchen pouring coffee and starting breakfast. "Oatmeal or cream of wheat?"

"Wheat."

"Peaches or pears?"

"Peaches."

"And how many eggs in your omelet?"

Lord, Stevie thought, what that man wouldn't eat. "I'll pass, thank you."

"I don't know, Stevie. I'm talking a *taco* omelet. Your favorite. All the fixings, cooked to a golden sheen, light and fluffy."

"One egg, no cereal," she conceded, because he did have a way with omelets. Even his infamous taco omelets turned out better than hers. Actually, everything he cooked turned out better. He used a lot more spices and a few ingredients like brown rice, expensive tropical fruits, and chinese stuff that she'd never eaten, but his meals always tasted good. Compliments, he'd told her, of his months as a river guide/cook in the backcountry of Alaska.

"I don't think I can make an omelet with one egg, won't be enough wrapper for all the stuff."

"Wing it." She took a sip of coffee and wondered how to mix up another cup with instant added without offending him—her biggest problem this morning. Life was good, even if she didn't know where it was all leading.

On his side of the kitchen Hal was having similar thoughts—about life, not food. Over the past couple of weeks he'd put a few feelers out around the world and had come up with a number of options. The Kioga brothers were putting together another assault of Dhaulagiri. They wouldn't depart the States until next spring, but if he wanted a slot, he'd have to get in on the ground floor and pull his weight with fund-raising and organization. A few months ago he would have gone for it without a doubt. But now—he glanced over his shoulder at Stevie—now he wasn't sure. He'd spent more hours of his life huddled in a snow cave or fighting his way up mountains than he'd spent loving her, and for all the magnetic pull of those high places, she pulled him harder.

Unlike most serious mountain climbers, he also had a reputation as a river runner, probably because he'd lived long enough to develop another interest. An offer had come in from George Jenkins for an attempt to float the Yangtze from its source. But Jenkins was an egomaniac, and Hal smelled doom and lots of bad karma around his latest scheme for immortality in the record books. And once again it meant leaving Stevie behind.

There still was Chauncey's place in Australia, but when he'd offered Stevie the trip, he hadn't planned on going with her; he hadn't planned on becoming so attached to her. But Australia wasn't one of his options; he knew he'd only be able to wrangle one plane ticket, Stevie's ticket. She had more than fulfilled her end of their bargain. She'd given him a job, and as she'd predicted, he'd earned his tax money before the Fourth of July. Backing out on his end of the deal never crossed his mind. No, in another month, she'd be trekking across the outback, and he'd be . . . what?

The ringing of the phone interrupted both their thoughts. Stevie reached out and flipped the receiver off the wall, catching it neatly on the down fall. Even half-asleep, her bartending skills were in good working order.

"Hello."

A long silence preceded the answer, then, sounding as if it came from the bottom of a deep well a voice said, "Person to person for a Mr. Halsey Morgan."

"It's for you," she informed him with an impressed lift of her brow. "Person to person."

Hal dried his hands on a dishtowel and threw it over his bare shoulder before taking the phone. "Halsey Morgan."

While he waited for the connection, Stevie moved over to the coffeepot and her hidden jar of instant coffee, thankful for the distraction—and curious as hell.

"Lola?"

Lola? She missed her cup with the second spoonful and her curiosity and her eyebrow shot up immediately.

"Slow down, honey. Take it easy. Start from the beginning."

Honey? He never called *her* honey. Her pang of jealousy was short-lived though. It faded as the grimness of his face increased.

"How long have they been missing? . . . Who else is up there? . . . Have you called Lars and Charlie? . . . Who's organizing the search and rescue operation? . . . Thanks for the vote of confidence." Stevie's heart sank lower with each question he asked. Then it hit bottom. "Have a plane ticket waiting for me at the Stapleton airport. I'll leave tonight. And Lola? Don't worry, sweetheart, I'll find your dad." He listened for a moment longer. "Okay. With luck, I'll see you the day after tomorrow."

Stevie's heart went beyond bottom. He was going to the other side of the earth. She'd always known he'd go, but not so soon, not that day.

With the receiver still tucked next to his ear and his finger on the disconnect lever, he glanced over at her. "Will you drive with me down to the airport?"

Silent and grief-stricken, she nodded.

He turned back to the phone and punched in the four digits of the local number. "Doug? . . . Hal. Stevie has to drive me to Denver today. Can you hold down the Trail? . . . Thanks. I'll buy you a beer when I get back . . . I don't know . . . Papua New Guinea . . . Yeah, it's a long way. See you."

Standing with her hands hanging at her sides, one of them clenched around a teaspoon, she waited for him to face her. When he did, she saw the lines of strain at the corners of his mouth, the tightness of his jaw, and the worry darkening his eyes—none of which came close to expressing the awful emptiness she felt.

"What happened?" she asked.

"Chauncey Keats has disappeared somewhere up the Waghi River. They found the rafts and pieces of equipment, but no bodies yet. That was his daughter Lola. She wants me to go in and try to find them."

"Them?" Stevie clutched the counter behind her. The gentle morning she'd awakened to suddenly had been catapulted into a roller coaster of crisis. Friends of Hal were missing, maybe hurt, possibly dead, and that left no time for the two of them, no time at all.

"He was leading the expedition, which was made up of experienced river runners, except for the eighteen-year-old boy who hired them. He happens to be the son of a very wealthy man. The old man is footing the bill for the search and rescue operation, and he wants the best." The inference was clear without being arrogant. When you were Halsey Morgan, you didn't need arrogance to make your point, she realized.

"How long have they been missing?" A hundred other questions teased the tip of her tongue, such as *What's going to happen to us? What will I do without you? Will you come back to me?*, but she didn't have the courage to ask them.

"A week. They started helicopter reconnaissance four days ago, but they really need a team down on the river. Can you finish breakfast while I get dressed? Then we'll go down to the cabin to pack. We have to stop somewhere before we get to the airport so I can pick up a few supplies."

"I'm not . . . uh . . . that familiar with Denver. I don't know where the big sporting goods stores are," she confessed, feeling incredibly foolish. Here he was, jetting off to the edge of the earth in a few hours without a second thought, and she didn't even know how to get around Denver.

"I don't need a sporting goods store, Stevie," he said with a quick smile. "A grocery store will do just fine."

"Grocery store?"

"Yes. I want a case of granola bars, nine or ten bottles of mosquito dope, and cheese spread."

"Cheese spread?" she repeated incredulously. What was going on?

"Maybe we'll get some of those little cans of pudding."

She stared at him for a long moment, confusion and concern narrowing her eyes and furrowing her brow. She started to say something then hesitated again, before finally getting up the nerve to ask. "Are you sure you know what you're doing?" She wouldn't even go on a three-day camping trip with cheese spread, pudding, and granola bars.

"First rule of the road, Stevie: Take your own

treats. You can get the basics anywhere. Lola wil
have them ready by the time I get there. She
provisions all her dad's expeditions."

Stevie bought his explanation, feeling as though
she'd just learned something useful—until they
got to his place and he started packing.

"That's it?"

"Maybe another pair of socks," he said, digging
into the pile of clothes strewn across his bed.

"But that's all you've got is socks!"

"Didn't I put in a pair of pants and four shirts?"

Stevie looked down into the flight bag in her
lap. "Well, yes."

"See if you can fit these in." He lobbed another
pair of socks over his shoulder, followed by under
wear and a couple of bandanas.

She diligently stuffed everything into the bag
and mused out loud, "I guess you'll take another
pack or something to carry the rest of your clothes."

"Nope,"—he dropped to his knees, reached un
der the bed, and pulled out a huge backpack cov
ered with zippers, pockets, and straps—"but I will
need this for the granola bars and my medical
kit."

The sight of the serious looking pack and his
mention of a medical kit eased her doubts a notch.
He knew what he was doing. In truth, he'd done it
a hundred times, taken off for the great unknown
on a moment's notice. Who was she to question
his gear?

She was the woman who loved him, came her
answer. Then she saw what she supposed was his
medical kit, a taped-together metal box with a
much faded red cross painted on top that was no
bigger than a paperback novel. She picked it up

and turned it over in her hands. The thing was ancient, scarred, dented—and she couldn't begin to imagine what lifesaving items might be stored in such a small tin.

Resigned to her curiosity, she peeled back the tape, dreading what she might or might not find. The box opened, and three Band-Aids floated to the floor.

Forcing her words to remain calm, she said, "Hal, I think you need to rethink your supply list. I mean, going off to New Guinea with a clean pair of socks, a jar of cheese spread, and three Band-Aids seems . . . well, it seems a little half-cocked."

Half-cocked? He silently mouthed the words, his head and shoulders still under the bed. "Did you know you're talking to the man who single-handedly organized four tons of gear for the Kioga brothers' only successful assault on Mount Everest?"

"No, I didn't." She paused for a moment, picking up the Band-Aids and giving them a doubtful look. "But I bet you took some aspirin."

"Ah hah." She saw him scoot farther under the bed. "Here, put these in the medical kit." One by one he handed her three brown plastic bottles, naming them as he went. "Anti-infection, anti-diarrhea, and anti—pain. That last one's the aspirin. Feel better?"

"Barely. What else have you got under there?" If he was going—and he was—she planned on making darn sure he had more than granola bars to keep him alive.

"Two water bottles." He put them behind him.

"How about a knife?"

"It's in my pocket."

If it was small enough to fit in his pocket, it wasn't big enough to ease her mind, but she kept silent on the point.

"Do you have a hat and some sunglasses?"

"Hat." He produced a beat-up stockman's hat. "My shades went down with the *Freedom*."

"Water purifying stuff?"

"Iodine's in the bathroom."

Stevie shot him a wry glance which was completely wasted on his rear end. "If you keep the iodine in the bathroom, why do you keep your other medicines under the bed?"

"I usually don't get intestinal bugs or headaches at home, but I've been known to cut a finger or two under the hood of my truck."

She had to ask, she thought, shaking her head in resignation.

"Any other requests while I'm under here?"

"A sleeping bag?"

"I'll get more use out of a mosquito net and a poncho." He rolled out. "Anything else?" he asked, sweeping a hand back through his hair.

Stevie looked around her at the things piled on the floor, knowing something was missing and yet unable to put her finger on it. "Money?" she voiced the obvious.

"We'll stop at the bank."

"I don't suppose you've got a gun."

"Never carry one, except in Alaska. But I know for a fact that I won't be needing to scare off many grizzlies in Papua New Guinea," he said with a quick grin.

Everything else she requested he supplied, and all of it fit in either his flight bag or the backpack, leaving plenty of room for his junk food, but no matter how she arranged it, it didn't look like enough. Something was still missing. . . .

"I'll be right back," she said abruptly, rising to her feet. Once outside the cabin she raced up the meadow to her house and up the stairs to her room. Nighties, teddies, and undies floated to the floor as she tossed them out of her dresser—until she found the object of her search. Sliding her fingers over the long, silver chain, she lifted the stone into her other hand. Nevada turquoise wasn't a South African diamond, and she'd never tested the luck of the piece, but it was all she had. Halsey Morgan was taking her heart into the middle of nowhere—he might as well take everything else.

When she returned to his cabin, he was back to rummaging around under the bed, but he'd added precious little to his pile of luggage.

"Found it!" he exclaimed, handing a small leather pouch up to her.

"What's this?"

"My compass."

"Thank God," she said, despite her best intentions not to let all of her doubts show.

Under the bed Hal winced. The woman's faith in him was downright demoralizing. "You do realize, don't you, Stevie, that I've managed to get around the world a couple of times on my own?"

"Yes. Yes, I know that, but I'm still worried." He heard the hesitation in her voice, and a grin spread across his face. This was a new feeling, a good feeling. He hadn't had anyone to worry about him since his parents had died, and even they had given up after awhile. But he didn't want Stevie Lee to ever give up on him, and he didn't want her to worry herself sick after he'd gone.

"And do you know"—he pushed out from under the bed and rolled to a sitting position, his knees spread, his hands resting in his lap—"do you know that nothing will keep me from coming back to you?" he asked, his rough voice adding depth and gentleness to the words.

Finally he'd told her what she really wanted to know. "I do now," she said softly. He was so beautiful, his hair slicked back from his shower, his shoulders broad and strong beneath his khaki shirt—and he was coming back to her. Kneeling down beside him, she leaned forward and slipped the necklace around his neck. "I don't know how lucky turquoise is, but my dad gave me this for my sixteenth birthday, and I've never been lost."

"It couldn't be because you've never been anywhere?" He winked, even as he pulled her into his arms.

"Don't tease me, Hal," she whispered. "I miss you already."

Holding her close with his arm draped around her shoulders, he studied the stone in his hand. "Thanks, Stevie. Looks like a pretty good piece of luck. I promise to take care of it."

"Just take care of yourself."

Cuddled up with her on the floor, he stroked her back and whispered his words of love and reassurance until all too soon it was time to go.

At the airport, they were sucked into a whirlwind of activity, picking up his ticket, checking his pack, and racing down the concourse.

"Lord, I'm sorry, Stevie," he said between long strides. "I thought she'd book me on the red-eye.

thought we'd have time to catch a bite to eat."
Near the security checkpoint he stopped and
wasted no time pulling her into his arms. Burying his head into the crook of her neck, he lowered his voice to a raspy drawl. "I thought we'd
have time for a long, painfully sweet good-bye."
With his hand cupping her chin, he gave her a
slow, burning kiss, his tongue sweeping her mouth
in lazy tracks.

Stevie clung to his neck, her hands tangling
through the long, blond hair laying across his
collar. Her body pressed against his in a vain
attempt to hold him forever, to sear the feel of
him irrevocably into her memory.

"Stay out of trouble." He laid a trail of kisses
along her jaw.

"Be careful, Hal," she whispered. "Please be
careful."

"Careful is my middle name." His mouth lingered on the curve of her ear, teasing the sensi-
tive skin and setting off small explosions of desire.
"I love you, Stevie Lee. Never doubt it, and never
forget it."

"Oh, Hal—" her voice broke with sadness.

He covered Stevie's mouth with one more hard
kiss, then he released her and started through
security. She watched him, her heart heavy, her
arms empty.

Suddenly he came back to the barrier. "Stevie,
catch!" He stopped and tossed a weighted envelope into the air. With a slight bend in her knees,
she caught it on the downfall. "My cabin and
truck keys. In case you need them. I love you!"

Before she had time to reply, he was gone. Standing with her mouth half-open and her breath

caught in her throat, she stared after him, hoping, yet knowing he wouldn't surprise her again. Slowly she looked down at the envelope holding the keys to all his worldly goods. Great, she thought, fighting back a tear. Now she had two houses and two cars to use and still no one to share them with. She wished just once the men in her life would stay put, instead of running off and leaving her a bunch of dubious assets.

Dubious assets? The thought startled her into looking up. Then, just as quickly, she looked down again and ripped open the envelope. Two smooth, worn keys slid into her hands along with one shiny new one—a safe deposit box key, she guessed. A feeling of dread and disbelief caused her hands to shake as she pulled out the single piece of folded paper inside.

Sweet Stevie Lee,
    I guess you'll be able to figure out which one of these opens the cabin and which one is supposed to, but probably won't, start the truck. My advice is—if I'm not back in a month, sell it and buy a new tire for Dynamite, maybe two if you get lucky.
    The other key is a bit trickier, and, yes, I can hear your mind working away even as this jet engine revs up. You taught me a lot this summer. How to love. How to tend bar. And the dangers of leaving unfinished business. I got lucky this time—I found you, and you were already taking care of my business pretty well. So I'm giving you another shot at it.
    If, and trust me, Stevie, this is a huge 'if—no one has ever won by taking the odds

against me and Mother Nature—if I'm not back in time to redeem my property, take the tricky key to Granby National Bank. In box number twelve you'll find enough cash to pay all the back taxes, but I don't recommend that course of action. You see, I learned a little bit about business from you too. If you redeem the property for me, and I don't come back, then it'll just sit there until the state claims it, and you'll end up looking down on a fast-food restaurant or something.

So I suggest you take enough of the cash to finish paying the taxes as you've done all along in your name. Then the property will be yours—the way it would have been if I'd never gotten off my piece of South Pacific paradise. Sell it, and go see all the places I've seen, all the places I want to take you. There's no one else I want to inherit the property, and there's never been anyone like you, Stevie. I suppose if we'd gotten married, we could have saved you a lot of paperwork—think about it.

All my love, Hal

Think about it? She didn't know whether to laugh or cry. Receiving a marriage proposal on the tail end of a last will and testament was as contrary to reason as—well, as surviving a shipwreck on a deserted island. Only Halsey Morgan could have pulled it off.

Clutching the letter to her breast, she bowed her head and started praying for his safekeeping right there in front of the security barrier. Partway through her fourth petition, her head snapped up. She needed the big guns. Ignoring the sidelong glances of a very confused airline employee, she dashed down the concourse to the first phone she saw.

Her foot tapped impatiently while she shovelled in the coins and waited for an answer on the other end. When the melodic, feminine voice answered, she felt a tremendous weight lift from her shoulders. "Mom, we've lost him to those pagan tropical lands again. Will you start praying now? I'll help when I get home."

Eleven

The first postcard came from Honolulu, Hawaii, the second from Sydney, Australia, and the third from the end of the earth—Kundiawa, Papua New Guinea. Stevie kept them all tucked into the shirt pocket next to her heart.

He'd been gone for a month, and despite her efforts, Stevie's memories were taking on a dreamlike quality: Hal smiling at her from the end of the bar, his golden mane of hair swept back from his face; Hal coming up behind her and softly kissing the top of her head, his hands automatically wrapping around her waist and drawing her close; and Hal loving her in the night, making her feel warm and sweet.

Autumn was coming early this year. Last week she'd seen elk in the lower pastures, and the aspens were turning copper, yellow, and orange.

"Stephanie?" The elderly lawyer's voice drew her attention back from the window to his desk. "One more signature and we're done," he assured her with a smile.

She looked down at the last contract and stared freedom in the face. One more flourish of the pen would unshackle her bonds. One more scribble would set her adrift. Was this what she really wanted? she asked herself for the thousandth time. No ties? No responsibilities? No job?

Six thousand dollars, a single payment, would be Stevie's with one more signature.

What was the old saying? Be careful what you wish for, because you might get it? Well, she'd spent half of her life wishing for the world, and each in their own way Kip and Hal were giving it to her. Kip by buying back his half of the bar with Brenda's money, and Hal with his vision, love, and spirit of adventure.

How much are you willing to risk? he'd asked her on a bright spring morning, and the reckoning time was now. She picked up the pen and signed her name in neat script. For Halsey Morgan she'd risk it all.

He'd been gone too long. He was too far away. And if—the *only* if she dared to entertain—he'd gotten himself lost again, she was going to find him. No one had bothered to organize a search party when he'd disappeared into the South Pacific. The cry of alarm hadn't gone up—but it echoed in her heart every hour of every day. She missed him with a dull ache that never left her.

"Better take this right over to the bank, Stephanie," Mr. Naish suggested, handing her the check. "And congratulations. I know your folks are glad to see you out from under the burden of running the Trail. Have you decided what you're going to do?"

"Yes. I'm going to take a vacation, to Papua New Guinea. I'm meeting a friend."

"Sounds adventurous. You must have been talking to that bartender you had working for you this summer. I've never met anybody who'd been to as many places as that boy, or anyone who could spin a yarn better. After a while, it got so his drinks weren't too bad either." He chuckled.

"Yes. He turned out okay," Stevie found herself agreeing impersonally. Mr. Naish might understand an exotic getaway, but she doubted if he'd approve of Richard and Elizabeth Carson's daughter chasing around the world after the man she loved.

"Well, good luck. Be sure and tell your dad I'll be coming up for a side of beef next week."

"I sure will, Mr. Naish. Thanks."

Stevie walked out of the lawyer's office and made a beeline for the Granby National Bank. Even more than selling the Trail, deciding what to do with Hal's property had caused her sleep-wrecking hours of thought. In the end, fighting off her superstitious instincts, she'd settled on the sensible thing. Hal had told her to take care of business, and that's exactly what she was going to do—no matter how awful it felt.

Two hours later she walked out of the county courthouse and headed home with a tax receipt made out to Stephanie Lisa Marie Brown burning a hole in her pocket. Now all she had to do was get her shots, her passport, and somehow find the courage to board a plane taking off into the great unknown.

Hal sat hunched over a table in the ramshackle

hotel lobby, sweat running down his face and chest. Using a finepoint pen, he marked in a few names and places on his map, places that hadn't been there before. He'd seen enough of Papua New Guinea in these last few weeks to hold him for a lifetime. But he had a friend in the cartography department at *National Geographic* who'd appreciate the new information.

The phone tucked between his shoulder and his chin crackled back to life, and he immediately grabbed it with his hand. "Lola? Can you hear me?"

"Loud and clear."

"Liar," he said, and heard her laughter bubble back at him. Loud and clear didn't exist between Kundiawa and Western Australia. "How's your dad?"

"Back on his feet and ready to go. He'll be in Kundiawa tomorrow afternoon to help out."

"Tell him to relax. We found the kid three days ago. He and his father left for the States this morning, and they took their lawsuit with them. Your dad is off the hook."

Hal had found Chauncey Keats and the other experienced river guides during the third week of the search. Finding the eighteen-year-old had taken quite a bit longer. Never in his years on the rivers of the world had Hal known someone to bolt into the jungle after a boat capsized. The kid must have been scared senseless. When they'd finally tracked him to a remote village, he still thought everyone else had died, drowned in the river.

One of the best things about finding the boy was getting his old man off everybody's back. He'd been spouting litigation drivel nonstop from the moment he'd arrived. He'd even threatened a few of the natives—as if they had anything he'd want. Hal had been sorely tempted to verbal, if not physical, violence many times, but now he was glad he'd held his temper. The old man had proven to be as generous in victory as he'd been abusive in defeat. Hal, Lars, and Charlie were all holding mighty fat checks for their days of grinding through the jungle.

"Lola, did you get that package put together and sent?"

"Plane tickets, itinerary, hotel accommodations, and a personal letter—the works. I mailed it first class, airmail, express, registered—everything I could think of. If Stevie Lee Brown wants to come down under, all she has to do is step out her front door."

"Backdoor."

"What?"

"She always leaves by the backdoor," Hal explained, a broad grin splitting his face.

"Well, as long as she leaves. I worked my tail off arranging her trip."

"Don't worry. She'll leave." *She'll be nervous, unsure, maybe even a little scared, but I know she'll leave—I know her. She'll take that first step into the world, whether I'm there to hold her hand or not.*

His lady with the big dreams never backed away from a challenge, be it a ton of hairy ape, a two-bit bar with no place to go but down, or the chance of a lifetime. "Make sure you're there to meet her at Denham. The airport looks a little empty to the uninitiated traveler."

"It'll take more than my presence to make that place look inhabited."

"Just be there. Did you sign the letter 'Love, Hal'?"

" 'Sincerely yours, Lola Keats,' is more my style."

"Keep in touch with Rocko so you know when he's dropping her off."

"I'm glad you mentioned that, Hal," the phone line went silent for a moment, then Lola continued hesitantly. "You know, I had to pull some pretty mean strings to get this whole shebang arranged. I don't think you have another favor left south of the equator. Dad says he's got you cornered this time for sure. What do you think about a partnership? Morgan and Keats Adventure Travel?"

"Well, you have the names in the right order, but I've got another partnership I need to work on first."

"Stevie Brown?" she asked, and when he confirmed it, she let out a long, low whistle. "Looks like the great Halsey Morgan is finally biting the dust, hitting the wall, losing his—"

"Right," he cut her off with a chuckle.

"What are you going to do if she doesn't show up?"

"That's easy, Lola." He pulled the long, silver chain out of his shirt and turned the turquoise cabochon over in his hand, watching the afternoon sunshine play across the aqua and green stone, remembering the sweet warmth of Stevie Lee's smile and the soft light of love in her eyes. "Real easy. I'm going to go get her."

Denham International Airport. Stevie read the sign, shaking her head in disbelief. They had to be kidding.

Four poles supporting a grass-hatched, chicken-wire roof baked in the sun. Miles of bare dirt and scrubby brush stretched to the horizon. The only amenities offered by the "international airport" were a Porta Potti and a low wooden bench. What was she doing there?

Sweating her guts out, and inhaling enough dust to choke a goat, came the obvious reply. Jamming her hands into her back pockets, she did a slow pirouette, scanning the desolation for a sign of life. She found only one: The retreating speck of Rocko's two-seater plane which had deposited her, bag and baggage, onto the hot, parched earth. Her first adventure was off to a precarious, panic-edged start. What *was* she doing here?

Actually things could be worse, she consoled herself. She could be stranded in Papua New Guinea. The thought alone buoyed her spirits. At least in Australia they spoke English, and cannibals hadn't been mentioned in any of her books and brochures.

The poor travel agent in Grand Lake had come darn close to tears when Stevie had raced into her office with a completely different trip already booked and paid for. The lady had worn out her phone lines just trying to find Kundiawa and arrange all the details necessary for such a journey. Clutching the big manila envelope to her chest, Stevie had apologized profusely, but she was sure the giddy smile on her face had made the agent doubt her sincerity. Stevie's feet barely had touched the ground since Lola's letter had arrived—until she'd landed in Australia.

Rocko's plane slowly disappeared into a ceru-

lean sky over an equally blue sea, and banked left
for the run back to Perth, leaving her on a spit of
land jutting into the Indian Ocean. Stevie pulled
the brim of her black Stetson lower on her forehead and turned back to the east. In front of her
the whole of Australia stretched for miles to the
Pacific, but Lola Keats had sent her to the desolate edge of the continent. And as far as she could
tell, she was alone with only a couple of flies for
company.

A tinkling sound drew her attention back to the
"airport." Hung from a wire, blowing in the wind,
a thermometer knocked against one of the metal
poles. Part of her mind said, "You don't want to
know." But curiosity pulled her forward. She'd
never felt anything like the heat burning up the
earth around her. She doubted if she could spit.

Dragging her canvas duffel bag behind her, she
stepped over to the thermometer and tilted her
head up.

"One hundred and two degrees," she whispered
aloud, not quite believing what she saw. With her
finger she tapped the instrument a few times,
seeing if the mercury would go down. It didn't. No
wonder she felt like a dried-out rag that had been
left on the line too long.

Wishing she hadn't looked, she pulled her hat
off and used her forearm to wipe away what little
sweat she had left. Lola was supposed to be meeting her. Stevie wished she'd show up. In truth
she wasn't sure how long she'd last. The blue
bandana tied around her neck and her white
T-shirt were stiff with dried perspiration, the cotton sleeves and the neck of the shirt stretched out
from her repeated tugging. Her khaki pants

though pleated to give her more room to maneuver, chafed her skin, and her brand new hiking boots felt like lead weights on her sweltering feet.

Ah, yes, she thought, her eyes scanning the horizon, adventure travel is a grand way to go. Back to the east, a wall of wind and dust was forming and heading to Denham, probably the only consistent visitor the place ever received. She hefted the bag to her shoulder and started for the Porta Potti, the best available protection. As she strode across the hard-baked earth, she settled her hat on her head and pulled the bandana up to cover her nose and mouth. Looking like a two-bit cattle rustler and feeling like the last lemming, she plopped herself down on the west side of the metal structure to wait out the windstorm.

The dust swirled up and around her narrow patch of sanctuary, caking the exposed mask of skin between her hat and her bandana, and adding a painful layer of grit to her sunburned cheeks. Heat off the tin wall broiled the back of her neck. A thin band of sweat formed under her hat.

The minutes turned into quarter hours, one after the other, until they made a whole hour, and still the wind blew and no one came. *What a place to die*—the thought came unbidden to her mind, rattling her waning composure. Days from now they'd find her desiccated body, a mere shrivel of her former self, clinging to a Porta Potti. She could see the hometown headline: STEVIE LEE FINDS HER TRUE TRAIL'S END—DIES IN A BATHROOM DOWN UNDER. Half the town would be wondering down under what? And the other half would be clicking their tongues and thinking, foolish girl, why did she go running off like that?

Why did she go running off? Try as she might, the answer eluded her. All the reasons she'd been accumulating for a lifetime, all the dreams, all the excitement, were slowly but surely being beaten out of her by the dry Western Australian wind.

What would Hal do in this situation? she wondered. Well, she figured, he'd probably make do, and she was doing that. He definitely wouldn't panic, and she was doing her darnedest not to. He might just get up and go, using his long legs, indomitable spirit, and his walking boots to find a better place. Stevie glanced down at her own boots and knew she wasn't going anywhere.

Squinting, she peered across the barren landscape and tried to hold her fears at bay. With effort she forced her mind to conjure up a vision of the Rocky Mountains: Blue-gray peaks pushing into the sky, pine-laden slopes cut through by fresh running streams, and glades of aspen sprinkled with the fairy flower columbine. Her eyes closed on the sweet memories, trying to make them real—a freshet of icy water flowing through her hands and numbing her fingers with its clear, pure coldness; the crispness of a late autumn breeze blowing across her brow and tangling her hair; the sound of a dust-choked engine crossing a dirt runway.

The wayward image drew her eyes open to narrow slits, and sure enough, she saw an approaching vehicle winding its way between the dust devils. Relief, pure and joyful, washed through her. She was saved.

Not wanting Lola to find her snuggled up to the bathroom, she pushed herself up to her feet and slapped the first two layers of dust off her pants.

Now stay cool, Stevie, she reminded herself. The last thing she wanted was to look like a frantic, overwrought tourist—which was exactly how she felt.

Standing with one hip thrown out to counterbalance the weight of the duffel slung over her shoulder, she held onto her hat and waited for the Jeep to reach her. Strands of her hair whipped around her head, tangling up and mingling with the windblown dirt. She pushed her hat lower and hefted the duffel higher, trying to create a windbreak.

The driver raised a hand in greeting, made a wild sweeping wave, actually, but it was all Stevie could do to waggle a few fingers away from their grip on the duffel strap.

"Come on, Lola, come on," she mumbled into her bandana, bracing herself against a heavy gust.

The Jeep lurched to a groaning stop and continued whining what Stevie instinctively knew was a death song. She knew it as surely as she was frying in the wind and the sun—and her heart plummeted back to her stomach. What could possibly go wrong next?

She didn't have to wait long for an answer. Before her very eyes, the hood of the Jeep blew back against the windshield, lifted by a rising plume of steam and water. The driver bailed out, and, fighting against the wind, made his way toward her.

No way did those broad shoulders belong to a lady named Lola, Stevie thought, watching the whole scene unfold like a bad dream—the steaming, dead Jeep in the background, a strange man bearing down on her, his head lowered, his stockman's hat jammed on low.

She started to back off when two things caught her eye: The flaxen glint of the hair under the hat, and the long sure stride eating up the distance between them. He walked like he owned the earth under his feet.

In a flash, she broke into a run.

Hal caught her up in his arms and twirled her around, kissing her ear, her temple, the bridge of her nose, every part of her left bare between her hat and bandana. Her fingers tunnelled through the hair sweeping around the collar of his chambray shirt, holding him as if she'd never let him go.

Slowly the initial thrill of seeing each other softened into something deeper, stronger. He lowered her back to her feet, his mouth following the retreating bandana as he tugged it away from her face, until his lips captured hers. The hot, yearning sweetness of his kiss went through her like a flame, searing her heart with tenderness and passion.

Never again, Hal promised himself. Never again would he leave without her. He needed this woman. He needed her life forever entwined with his. He needed her body and her love to make him whole—and the lazy, searching track of her mouth beneath his, the tightness of her arms around his neck, her very presence told him of her needs.

He would have kissed her until the sun fell into the ocean, until the moon rose above the desert, but the increasing tempo of the storm forced a distracting level of common sense upon them both.

"Jeep," he said close to her ear, and felt her nod. Pulling her under his arm for protection, he guided her to the driver's side of the vehicle and helped her inside.

Through the side window, Stevie watched him go back for her duffel bag, all of her fears banished and replaced by a new and wondrous sense of adventure. The other side of the world, however barren and scorched, looked like paradise with Hal at her side. The dust storm became a wild veil of mystery over the landscape, the sun's heat a display of Mother Nature's intense charms. As for the dead Jeep, now it was a mere inconvenience, the problem of the moment. She'd seen Hal in action on his truck engine, and her faith in his skill knew no bounds. He'd have them purring along through the outback in no time. Then they could talk and talk and talk. She wanted to hear his latest hair-raising story about the search, and she'd promised all the folks back home a long, detailed letter including every dangerous twist. But most of all, she wanted to talk about the letter he'd given her the day he'd left. She'd had plenty of time to think and had needed none of it. The night he'd walked into the Trail, she'd felt her life change course, and no matter how hard she'd fought against it, her life had continued to change and change. All she had to do was look out the window to see how far she'd come and to look into her heart to know how much he'd given her. A fresh wave of happiness brought a smile to her mouth.

An hour later, as she munched on a ham sandwich, she realized the happiness still hadn't deserted her. The storm had long since passed them by, but they hadn't budged an inch, and she still wasn't worried. In her mind she saw days like this stretching out timelessly into the future. No clocks to punch, no ledger books weighing her down, just she and Hal discovering the wild places. She'd take it for as long as she could get it. She had a lot of her own wanderlust bottled up inside, and he'd popped the cork.

"Okay, Stevie, crank her up," he hollered from underneath the hood. "Heavy on the gas."

One foot firm on the clutch, the other playing the gas pedal, she turned the key. While she listened for the engine to catch, she helped herself to a long swallow of lukewarm tea out of the water bottle.

"Stop!"

She turned off the key and exchanged the bottle for the sandwich in her lap. Chewing away contentedly, she waited for his next command.

"Start."

She did.

"Stop."

She did.

"Sandwich."

She leaned way out the window and giggled as he devoured the sandwich out of her hand, leaving her only the little bit grasped in her fingers.

"Thanks," he mumbled, disappearing under the hood again. "Okay, this is it. Now or never."

Stevie popped the rest of the sandwich in her mouth, sent up a prayer, and turned the key. Slowly the engine puttered to life.

Grinning from ear to ear, he peeked out from under the hood and gave her the thumbs-up sign. They were back in business. He slammed the hood down and came around to the passenger side.

"You better drive," he explained, with a warm

smile deepening the creases in his dust-caked face. "I don't think I can take my eyes off you."

"I feel the same way about you," she admitted softly, feeling all of her love well up inside her.

"Well, if I start in now telling you how much I missed you, we'll still be here next week—and I've got other plans for tonight."

"Such as?"

"Camping under the stars. I want you all to myself for a few days before we head back to Chauncey and Lola's."

"Umm. Sounds nice." Her eyes twinkled mischievously.

"How about cooking out over an open fire?"

"Sounds even better."

"Skinny-dipping in a borehole?"

Tossing her braid over her shoulder, she laughed and jimmied the gearshift into first. "You're on. Which way?"

Hal slipped a compass out of his shirt pocket and held it flat in his hand. With his other hand he pointed out her side of the windshield. "Southeast. I know a shortcut. We'll pick up another road ten miles from here."

Stevie watched him slide the compass into a slot on the dashboard, fighting to keep a small, twitching grin off her face. He leaned over and gave her a smacking kiss, then flopped back in his seat.

"Lord, I'm glad to see you. Let's go before we cook in here."

Pushing her hat to the back of her head, she slanted him a dry look and said, "Shortcut, Hal? One of *your* shortcuts?"

Slouched against the door, he pushed his own

hat back and met her gaze directly. A broad, easy
smile slowly spread across his face and crinkled
the corners of his deep blue eyes. "I can tell right
now you're gonna make my life a lot more interesting."

"Coming from you, that's quite a compliment."

"I meant it to be." He nodded in agreement,
then reached over and tapped the compass. "Southeast, Stevie, and I'll have you floating up to your
neck in cool green water before the sun goes down."

"Promises, promises," she said, pulling her hat
down and easing off the clutch.

Driving along the roadless track, she listened as
he told her about his days in the jungle, where
he'd searched high and low for a frightened
eighteen-year-old boy. His gravelly voice expressed
every nuance of the adventure. Stevie gasped in
all the right places and held her breath through
others, reliving the tale with him.

Hal watched the emotions cross her face, loving
the natural way she showed her feelings. All the
time he talked he kept his arm across the back of
her seat, continually touching her shoulder or
letting his thumb brush along the side of her
neck. More than once, she pulled over so they
could kiss and murmur their words of love.

Just before dusk, Stevie spotted the skeletal
form of a windmill shimmering on the horizon,
its base seemingly disconnected from the ground.
"Another fifteen minutes and—"

"And you'll be up to your neck in water. Go
ahead and strip down." He gave her a sly wink.

"I'll be moving too fast for you to see much," she
said. With a flick of her wrist she tossed her hat
into the back of the Jeep. She unknotted her

bandana and sent it flying behind her hat, and even as she braked to a stop, she was pulling her T-shirt out of her pants.

Hours later under a full moon and a sky resplendent with stars, she lay in Hal's arms, feeling well fed, well loved, and infinitely at peace with her big, new world.

"So what's the news from home?" He levered himself up on to his elbow and gazed down at her, his free hand gently brushing the hair back from her face. Light from the camp fire flickered and danced over the tawny goldness of his hair and the hard angles of his body, tracing the breadth of his shoulders, adding shadow to the muscles in his arms.

Stevie stretched out beside him and tucked her hands beneath her head. "Well, Diana had a little girl. Mom is thrilled, and whipping up pink dresses as fast as her old sewing machine can go. Kip and Brenda got married last month, and I signed the Trail back to him. He paid me in cash, the whole six thousand. I'm loaded. You might want to keep me around for a while."

"Maybe," he said, flashing one of his midnight smiles.

She was right, Stevie thought. She loved finding his head on the pillow next to hers when the world was dark and quiet. And he never failed to whisper something passionate and foreign when they made love.

"More than maybe," she said innocently.

"I assume you're talking about my unfinished business."

"Yep."

"I knew this was going to be interesting." He waited a moment for her to tell him what she'd done. But all she did was lay there looking beautiful and slightly smug. "Come on, Stevie. Don't keep me hanging."

She gave him a laconic glance, letting a small smile flirt with her mouth, then said, "You still own the truck."

Letting out with a loud groan, he rolled over on his back and threw an arm over his face. "Oh, brother. I guess this means I'll have to marry you."

"There's no guess about it," she said calmly, stretching her left hand out in front of her. "A small gold band will do."

"A small gold band? How small?" He lifted his head hopefully.

"Oh, about an eighth of an inch."

"You've given this a lot of thought, haven't you?" he asked, reaching for his pants.

"Not much, actually."

"Well, then I guess you won't be disappointed with this." He pulled a piece of tissue paper out of his pocket and tossed it on the bedroll. Stevie picked it up and felt something hard wrapped inside. Her eyebrows rose. He continued. "The band is actually closer to a quarter inch, but I'm sure I can have somebody knock off—"

"A diamond!" Stevie stared at the huge, uncut stone mounted on a heavy ring of gold. "Oh, Hal . . ." her voice trailed off softly.

"Is that 'Oh, Hal' a yes?"

"It's so big." She turned the ring this way and that, letting the fire shine through the chunk of gem. "I've never seen anything like it."

"We can have it cut and polished if you like . . . if you say yes."

"Oh, Hal, no, not this stone. We don't dare chip anything off my good luck charm. Besides, I think I like my diamonds the same way I like my men"—she glanced up at him from under her lashes, her eyes shy and soft—"kind of rough around the edges."

He grinned and slowly drew her over on top of him. "That has to be a yes, because I'm as rough as they come," he said. Then, for the rest of the night, he proved only how gentle he was, loving her with tenderness and care.

Twelve

"Morgan, Keats, Morgan, and Keats," Hal read the letterhead aloud, a wry grin curving his mouth. "We sound like a law firm. Can't you ladies come up with something a little less redundant? You know what the guides are calling us, don't you?"

"They call me boss. I can just imagine what they call you." Stevie searched through the mess on her desk, finally coming up with the right file folder.

"They call us Mickey Mick, which is damn close to Mickey Mouse, which is a hell of a moniker for an agency with our safety record. And they may call you boss in here, but everywhere else they call you Trouble. From the Andes to Alaska, they know Trouble is watching them like a hawk." He didn't dare tell her they also called her "Legs," and it wasn't because she kept up with the best of them. She already knew she had the guides wrapped around her fingers.

"Those boys are wild. They need someone to keep an eye on them."

Hal's smile broadened as he watched her rummage around for a pencil. "It's stuck behind your ear."

"Oh, thanks, sweetheart." She pulled the pencil out and began jotting notes on the folder. "I'll be done here in a minute, then we can go home."

"It's Sunday," he reminded her, and saw a smile of relief touch the corners of her mouth.

"Great," she said with a sigh, relaxing back in her chair. "Dinner at Mom and Dad's. We don't have to cook."

"You mean I don't have to cook." He'd become a regular house husband since their marriage, at least during the few months out of the year when they were home. "How's the O'Neill trip coming along?"

"I've got them booked through the Great Barrier Reef, and Lola's picking them up for the outback tour. My problem is with the Hobarts in Sydney. They decided to add an extra week to their vacation, and they want to spend it rafting the Colorado through the Grand Canyon. On such short notice I'm having a heck of a time fitting them on a raft."

With the Morgans on one side of the equator and the Keats on the other, and Chauncey's and Hal's—especially Hal's—reputations backing them up, their travel agency and outfitting service had taken off like a rocket. During the course of her dealings and travels, Stevie had racked up a few favors owed her, but something as simple as this Grand Canyon problem left her stymied. She'd been to Alaska, South America, and Australia, but she'd never been to Arizona.

"Didn't Johnny used to make that run?" Hal asked, referring to one of their guides.

"Of course! He has all kinds of connections down there." She leaned forward and started dialing. "Why didn't I think of that?"

"Because I'm the brains behind this operation. I just keep you around to look at."

"Hah!" She laughed and slanted a teasing glance up at him. "You'd be lost without me."

Before her finger hit the last button, Hal took the phone receiver out of her hand and set it back in its cradle. "Business can wait." He grasped her hand in his, pulling her out of the chair and into his arms.

Stevie went willingly, the Hobart file spilling out of her lap and onto the floor. "Now look what you made me do," she whispered, wrapping her arms around his neck. "The Hobarts will probably end up in their own backyard instead of the Grand Canyon." Her fingers tunnelled through the flaxen length of his hair, which no amount of growth had been able to darken down; he still spent most of his days in the sun. And he spent all of his nights in her arms. Wherever he went, she was by his side, be it the wild rivers of Alaska, or the ancient ruins of Peru.

"Then Lola will show them a part of it they never dreamed existed," he said, settling her against him with a mischievous grin. "I've got a present for you."

Caught by the underlying thread of excitement in his voice, she lifted her face in expectation. "Present?"

With the gentleness of love, he smoothed his hand across the side of her face, sliding the ever-wayward strands of loose, honey-brown hair behind her ear. His voice lowered to a rough timbre. "Do you know how I love you, Stevie?"

"The way I love you," she answered slowly, softening against him, molding her body to his and touching her fingers to his cheek. She loved him the way the flowers loved the sun, the way the sea loved the shores. He had opened her to the world, letting her blossom in the light; he was her home at the end of each day's journey, always there, never wavering.

"The way all men have loved the other half of their hearts," he continued. "Everything I have is yours, but like you figured out long before you met me, financial security isn't my long suit."

Gazing at him through eyes filled with love, she shook her head in disagreement. Truthfully he'd given her more security than she'd ever hoped to have, not only financially—their business was booming—but emotionally, which was his greatest gift.

"Ah, you're good to me, Stevie. Good *for* me."

"And that is why"—she kissed the side of his mouth—"you bring me presents."

"Actually I didn't bring the present to you." At the immediate lift of her brow, he explained further. "It's so big I'll have to take you to the present."

"There's a story in this somewhere, isn't there?" The question was rhetorical. She knew how his mind worked; it worked up a story at the drop of a pin, and a present too big to deliver was an opportunity she knew he wouldn't pass up.

She was right.

"There once was a man," he began, his smile fading, "a very wealthy man, who loved a woman; Shah Jehan was his name. The woman was called Mumtaz Mahal, 'Splendour of the Palace,' an ebony-haired, dark-eyed beauty who held his heart in her hand. But she couldn't have been more beautiful than you, Stephanie Lisa Marie, and not even a Mogul emperor could love you as much as I do." He paused and sealed his pledge with a soft kiss. Then his mouth traced a gentle line to her ear, where he lingered as he wove his magic tale, holding her close. "When she died and darkness seemed to be all around the Shah, he built a rare palace born to capture the dawn, a monument to love in opalescent marble. The *Taj Mahal* floats in the early morning light, a blessing for all to see, like your first waking smile, Stevie. She stands untouched by the storms of time, like my love. I want to take you there, to Agra, to say good-bye to our first year together and to celebrate the years to come. Say yes, and we'll leave the day after tomorrow."

Overcome by the depth of his emotions and her own, Stevie could only nod her acceptance. She could only send up a heartfelt prayer of thanks to the Lord for always keeping him safe and bringing him back to her. She could only hold him tighter and whisper, "I love you, Halsey Morgan."

THE EDITOR'S CORNER

Next month we celebrate our sixth year of publishing LOVESWEPT. Behind the scenes, the original team still works on the line with undiminished enthusiasm and pride. Susann is a full editor now, Nita is still the "fastest reader in the East or West," Barbara has written every single piece of back-cover copy (except the three I wrote in the first month, only proving Barbara should do them all), and from afar Elizabeth still edits one or two books each month. And I believe I can safely say that our authors' creative contributions and continuing loyalty to the line is unparalleled. From book #1 (**HEAVEN'S PRICE** by Sandra Brown) to book #329 (next month's **WAITING FOR LILA** by Billie Green) and on into the future, our authors consistently give us their best work and earn our respect and affection more each day.

Now, onward and upward for at least six more great years, here are some wonderful LOVESWEPT birthday presents for you. Joan Elliott Pickart leads off with **TO FIRST BE FRIENDS,** LOVESWEPT #324. Shep Templeton was alive! The award-winning journalist, the only man Emily Templeton had ever loved, hadn't died in the Pataguam jungle, but was coming home—only to learn his wife had divorced him. Eight months before, after a night of reckless passion, he had left for his dangerous assignment. She'd vowed then it was the last time Shep would leave her. Love for Emily was all that had kept Shep going, had made him want to live through months of pain and recovery. Now he had to fight for a new start. . . . Remember, this marvelous book is also available in a beautiful hardcover collector's edition from Doubleday.

In **BOUND TO HAPPEN,** LOVESWEPT #325, by Mary Kay McComas, a breathtaking angel drives Joe Bonner off the road, calls him a trespasser, then faints dead away in his arms. Leslie Rothe had run away from her sister's wedding in confusion, wondering if she'd ever fall

(continued)

in love—or if she even wanted to. Joe awakened turbulent emotions, teased her unmercifully, then kissed her breathless, and taught a worldly woman with an innocent heart how it felt to love a man. But could she prove how much she treasured Joe before her folly destroyed their love?

Next, we introduce an incredibly wonderful treat to you. Deborah Smith begins her Cherokee Trilogy with **SUNDANCE AND THE PRINCESS,** LOVESWEPT #325. (The second romance in the trilogy, **TEMPTING THE WOLF,** will be on sale in June; the final love story, **KAT'S TALE,** will be on sale in August.) In **SUNDANCE AND THE PRINCESS** Jeopard Surprise is Robert Redford gorgeous, a golden-haired outlaw whose enigmatic elegance enthralls Tess Gallatin, makes her want to break all the rules—and lose herself in his arms! He'd come aboard her boat pretending to court the blue-eyed Cherokee princess, but his true mission—to search for a stolen diamond—was endangered by Tess's sweet, seductive laugh. Tess could deny Jep nothing, not her deepest secrets or her mother's precious remembrance, but she never suspected her lover might betray her . . . or imagined how fierce his fury might blaze. An incandescent love story, not to be missed.

LOST IN THE WILD, LOVESWEPT #327, by Gail Douglas, features impossibly gorgeous Nick Corcoran, whose mesmerizing eyes make Tracy Carlisle shiver with desire. But her shyness around her grandfather's corporate heir apparent infuriates her! For three years Nick had considered her off limits, and besides, he had no intention of romancing the snobbish granddaughter of his powerful boss to win the top job. But when Tracy outsmarted a pair of kidnappers and led him into the forest in a desperate escape plan, Nick was enchanted by this courageous woodswoman who embraced danger and risked her life to save his. But could Tracy persuade Nick that by choice she wasn't his rival, only his prize?

(continued)

Peggy Webb gives us pure dynamite in **ANY THURS-DAY**, LOVESWEPT #328. Hannah Donovan is a sexy wildcat of a woman, Jim Roman decided as she pointed her rifle at his chest—definitely a quarry worthy of his hunt! With a devilish, devastating smile, the rugged columnist began his conquest of this beautiful Annie Oakley by kissing her with expert, knowing lips . . . and Hannah felt wicked, wanton passion brand her cool scientist's heart. Jim wore power and danger like a cloak, challenged and intrigued her as few men ever had—but she had to show him she couldn't be tamed . . . or possessed. Could they stop fighting destiny and each other long enough to bridge their separate worlds? A fabulous romance!

Remember Dr. Delilah Jones? In **WAITING FOR LILA**, LOVESWEPT #329, Billie Green returns to her characters of old for a raucous good time. Lila had special plans for the medical conference in Acapulco—this trip she was determined to bag a husband! She enlisted her best friends as matchmakers, invited them to produce the perfect candidate—rich, handsome, successful—then spotted the irresistibly virile man of her dreams all by herself. Bill Shelley was moonstruck by the elegant lady with the voice like raw silk, captivated by this mysterious, seductive angel who seemed to have been made just for him. Once he knew her secrets, could Bill convince her that nothing would keep her as safe and happy as his enduring love? A pure delight from Billie!

Enjoy!

Carolyn Nichols

Carolyn Nichols
Editor
LOVESWEPT
Bantam Books
666 Fifth Avenue
New York, NY 10103